Enola
HOLMES

THE CASE OF THE BIZARRE BOUQUETS

ALSO BY NANCY SPRINGER

Enola HOLMES

THE CASE OF THE BIZARRE BOUQUETS

Nancy Springer

HOT
KEY
BOOKS

First published in Great Britain in 2021 by
HOT KEY BOOKS
4th Floor, Victoria House
Bloomsbury Square, London WC1B 4DA
Owned by Bonnier Books
Sveavägen 56, Stockholm, Sweden
www.hotkeybooks.com

This is a work of fiction. Names, places, events and incidents are either
the products of the author's imagination or used fictitiously. Any
resemblance to actual persons, living or dead, is purely coincidental.

A CIP catalogue record for this book is available from the British Library.

ISBN: 9781471410789
also available as an ebook

2

This book is typeset using Atomik ePublisher
Printed and bound in Great Britain by Clays Ltd, Elcograf S.p.A.

www.bonnierbooks.co.uk

To my mother

MARCH,
1889

LUNATICS HAVE NO COMMON SENSE, thinks the matron, but then, that's what deranges the faculties, isn't it, lack of common sense? Take this new inmate now: If he had any sense, he would be exercising with the others in the airing yard on this beautiful sunny day, the first fine day of spring; he'd be following directions ("Stand up straight! Breathe deeply! Lift your eyes and contemplate the glories of the firmament! Now, march! Left foot first, ONE-two-three-four!") and he'd be doing himself some good, but instead—

"Let me out," he demands for perhaps the hundredth time. "I am an *Englishman*! Such treatment of a British citizen simply cannot be tolerated." While his tone is angry, he doesn't curse, she'll give him that; even at his worst, when he fought with the keepers, when he blackened the director's eye, even then he hadn't cursed. Nor does he now, only complaining vehemently, "Let me out. I demand my rights as a loyal subject of the Queen. Let me out of this confounded coffin, I say!"

"It's not a coffin, Mr. Kippersalt." Sitting in a comfortless wooden chair, cushioned only by her own amplitude while in her lap she knits a sock, the matron speaks in a bored but soothing tone. "The top and bottom resemble those of a coffin, perhaps, but you know quite well that a coffin would not have spindlework all up and down the sides so you can breathe and I can see that you are not in any difficulties—"

"Not in any difficulties?" Unexpectedly, the man lying in the confines of the restraining box starts to laugh. At the sound of his laughter the matron drops a stitch, frowns, and lays her knitting aside, reaching for paper and pencil instead.

"Not in any *difficulties* in this fiendish device?" the man cries amidst unnaturally high-pitched yowls of laughter.

"You do not appear to be physically indisposed," answers the matron with gentle dignity, "and you are lying on a clean pallet, and you can change your position, move your hands. Certainly the crib is preferable to a straitjacket."

"A crib! Is *that* what it's called?" The man is still laughing for no good reason. The matron watches him narrowly, knowing she must take care with him; he was quite unexpectedly quick for such a stocky fellow, and resourceful, too. He very nearly made it to the fence.

In Mr. Kippersalt's barely started casebook she writes the date and time, then, *Patient laughing in apparent hysteria.* Earlier notations state that Mr. Kippersalt most strenuously resisted putting on his grey woollen uniform while his own things were taken away for safekeeping; that he has refused food; that his urine is light and clear, he moves his bowels appropriately, and he seems to be of a cleanly nature; that he shows no deformity of the head, trunk, or limbs; that he exhibits intelligence of a sort, and that he uses a handkerchief.

"A crib, as in, cheating me of my freedom?" The man's unnerving laughter is quietening. Not a bad-looking man of middle age, a soldierly type, he strokes his moustache with his fingers as if to calm himself, or to think. "When are you going to let me out?"

"After the doctor has looked you over." After first administering chloral hydrate, the matron feels sure. Himself an addict to laudanum and the like, the asylum's doctor troubles himself little with the inmates other than to medicate them.

"Doctor? I *am* a doctor!" The newly committed lunatic starts once again to howl with laughter.

The matron writes, *Persists in his grandiose delusions.* Setting the casebook aside, she takes up her knitting again. Trying to turn the heel of a sock can be most vexing, but that's the way things are when one is married to the director of a lunatic asylum: always seven things to do at once, never a quiet moment to simply rest one's soul, go for a walk or look at a newspaper. The nurses require as much supervision as the patients do; Florence Nightingale's influence has not extended here, and the help is illiterate at best, if not in the grip of some vice, usually drink.

The matron sighs. Trying to pick up the stitch she dropped, she cannot keep a slight edge from creeping into her voice as she replies, "A doctor? That's not true, Mr. Kippersalt.

Your documents of admission clearly state that you are a shopkeeper."

"My name is not Kippersalt! I am not the person you say I am! Why can I not make anyone at this hellish place understand that I am here because of some absurd misapprehension?"

Feeling the man watching her from the coffin-like box in which he lies, the matron smiles, albeit wearily. "In my experience of the past thirty years, Mr. Kippersalt, patients very often believe a mistake has been made, but it has never been so." How could it be, when such considerable sums of money have changed hands? "Take gentlemen like you, now. A number have come here declaring themselves to be Napoleon—that's the most frequent, but we've had a Prince Albert, a Sir Walter Drake and a William Shakespeare—"

"I'm telling you the *truth*!"

"—and some of those poor distracted minds are eventually cured," the matron speaks on, ignoring the interruption, "but some of them remain here yet. Is that what you want, Mr. Kippersalt? To remain here for the rest of your life?"

"My name is not Kippersalt! It's Watson!" Even through the spindles she can see his moustache bristling.

With kindly whimsy she retorts, "We have a Sherlock Holmes in one of the other wards. I wonder whether he would care to vouch for you."

"You are mad! I tell you, I *am* John Watson, medical doctor and author! All you have to do is telephone Scotland Yard—"

Telephone? As if anyone this far north of London City

has ever seen or used such a come-lately contraption? Just call Scotland Yard? Grandiose delusions again.

"—and ask for Inspector Lestrade. He will confirm my identity—"

"Nonsense," the matron murmurs. "Nonsense." He really thinks the director will make inquiries, give back a considerable fee and turn him loose? The man is raving. "Shush now. Shhh." As if trying to calm a child, she murmurs to him, concerned; such passion might lead to brain fever if it does not soon abate. It has been two days now and Mr. Kippersalt is still ranting just as irrationally as he was when they brought him in. A sad case, really. The matron has dealt with many lunatics, but she feels particularly sorry for this one, because he seems as if he might have so much good in him if he were in his right mind.

CHAPTER
THE
FIRST

IT IS DIFFICULT TO CHOOSE A NEW name for oneself. Even more difficult, I imagine, than choosing a name for a child, for one is confusingly intimate with oneself, whereas one is barely acquainted with a baby upon its arrival. Some artistic whim, surely, had caused Mother to name me "Enola," which, backwards, spells *alone.*

Do not think about Mother.

Although the large bruise on my face had faded, the even larger one upon my feelings had not. Thus I remained in my lodging on the first fine, sunny day in March, 1889. With paper and pencil in hand, I sat at my open window (how welcome is fresh air—even the London variety—after a long winter!) looking out over the seething East End street. The scene below had attracted my attention: Due to a quantity of mutton still on the hoof passing through, all manner of vehicles, including coal-wagons, donkey-carts and costermongers' barrows, had locked shafts; I could hear the drivers shouting the most frightful oaths at one another. Red-coated army recruiters and other idlers looked on, grinning, while a blind beggar led by a ragged child tried to get past the jam, street urchins climbed lampposts to stare and jeer, and women in sooty shawls hurried on their errands.

They—the sorely overworked women of the slums—unlike me, had somewhere to go.

Looking down on the paper in my lap, I found that I had written:

Enola Holmes

Hastily and heavily I crossed out this, my very own name, the one I absolutely could not use. My brothers Mycroft and Sherlock, you see, must not find me, for they quite wanted to take charge of me and transform me, via singing lessons and similar vapours, into an ornament for genteel society. Which, legally, they could do. Force me into boarding school, I mean. Or into a convent, an orphanage, a Young Ladies' Academy of Porcelain Painting, wherever they chose. Legally, Mycroft, the elder, could even have me locked up for life in an insane asylum. Such confinement required only the signature of two medical doctors, one of whom would be the "mad doctor" who quite wanted money to run the place. Those, and the signature of Mycroft himself—any scheme to deprive me of my freedom I would not put beyond him.

I wrote:

The name I had used during the six months I had been a fugitive, on my own. "Ivy" for fidelity, "Meshle" a play on "Holmes"—*Hol mes, mes Hol, Meshle*—and I liked that name; I really wished I could keep it. But I was afraid—I had discovered that Sherlock knew I used Ivy as a code name when communicating with Mother through the newspaper personal columns.

What else did my oh-so-clever brother Sherlock—the one who, as opposed to the large and sessile Mycroft, was actually on the hunt for me—what did Sherlock know about me? What had he learned in the course of our most irregular dealings?

I wrote:

He knows I look like him. He knows I climb trees.
He knows I ride a bicycle.
He knows I disguised myself as a widow.
He knows I disguised myself as a poor woman selling pen-wipers.
He knows I disguised myself as a nun.
He knows I gave food and blankets to the poor.
He knows I carry a dagger in my corset.
He knows I have located two missing persons.
He knows I have put the police onto two villains.
He knows I have twice invaded his Baker Street rooms.
He knows I use the name Ivy.

One must assume that he now knows from Dr. Watson
that a young woman named Ivy Meshle worked for
the world's first and only Scientific Perditorian.

I sighed at this last, for I quite admired Dr. Watson, although I had encountered the good physician only three times: the first when he had come to consult the Perditorian—a professional seeker of missing persons—for the sake of his friend Sherlock Holmes; the second when I had gone to ask him a question and he had given me a bromide for a headache; the third when I had thrust an injured lady upon his care. Dr. Watson was the epitome of a gallant, sturdy English gentleman, willing to help anyone. I liked him tremendously, almost as much as I liked my brother—for, despite everything, I did adore Sherlock, although I knew him mainly through the very popular stories his friend Watson wrote about him, which I read as avidly as anyone in England.

Why, why did those for whom I cared always seem to prove my undoing?

Sighing, I pressed my lips together and drew several heavy pencil lines crossing out *Ivy Meshle*.

What, then?

It was not just choosing a new name that baffled me; it was the all-encompassing problem of what to do and whom to be. Within what sort of woman should I next hide myself? A commoner, Mary or Susan? How dull. Yet the flower names I loved, such as Rosemary, symbol of remembrance, or Violet, symbol of hidden beauty and virtue, were out of the question, for Sherlock knew about the code Mother and I used.

Nor could I fall back upon one of my middle names; I had, of course, the usual gentrified quota of them, being christened Enola Eudoria Hadassah Holmes. Enola E. H. Holmes—E.E.H.H. Eehh. Just the way I felt. Hadassah being my father's deceased sister's name, which Sherlock would instantly recognise, and Eudoria, even worse, being my mother's given name.

Not that I cared in any way to style myself after my mother. Or did I?

"Curses! Ye gods," I muttered naughtily, writing down.

Violet Vernet

Vernet being my mother's maiden name, which, again, Sherlock Holmes would recognise at once. But perhaps backwards?

Tenrev

Well, no. But if I played with the letters a bit?

Netver
Never
Every
Ever

Ever what?
Ever alone?
Ever forlorn?

Ever defiant, I told myself sternly. *Ever to go on being—what I am.* A rebel, a dreamer, and a perditorian, finder of the lost. It occurred to me that, as a step in that direction, in order to hear news that did not reach print, I ought to try to find a position with some Fleet Street publication—

Coincidentally, as I thought this I heard my landlady's tortoise-like tread upon the stairs. "Newspapers, Miss Meshle!" she bellowed even before she had reached the landing. Being as deaf as a turnip, Mrs. Tupper seemed to find it necessary to make a great deal of noise.

As I stood up, crossed my room and threw everything I had written into the fire, she knocked hard enough to crack walnuts. "Newspapers, Miss Meshle!" she shouted into my face just as I opened the door.

"Thank you, Mrs. Tupper." She couldn't hear me, of course, but she could see my lips move in what I hoped was a smile as I took the papers from her hands.

However, she did not then go away. Instead, she straightened her short, hunched form to its limit and fixed me with her watery gaze. "Miss Meshle," she declaimed with the bravado of one who has decided to perform a Moral Duty, "it's no good yer shuttin' yerself up this way. Now whatever 'appened, and it's none of my business, but whatever it was, it's no use gittin' pale about. Now, it's a nice day out, wit' a bit uv sun and startin' to feel springish. Now whyn't you git yer bonnet on an' go out for a walk, at least—"

Or I believe she said something of the sort. I barely heard her, and I am sorry to say I shut the door in her face, for my gaze had caught upon the *Daily Telegraph*'s headline and fixed there.

It said:

*SHERLOCK HOLMES ASSOCIATE
MYSTERIOUSLY DISAPPEARS
DR. WATSON'S WHEREABOUTS UNKNOWN*

CHAPTER
THE
SECOND

NOT PAUSING EVEN TO TAKE A SEAT, but standing where I was, with the skirt of my cheap cotton at-home dress nearly in the fire, I read:

Events sure to send a frisson of horror through any spine with delicacy of feeling have unfolded in Bloomsbury, with implications taking in the whole of London, if a missing British gentleman is not soon found. Dr. John Watson, a respected physician perhaps best known as companion of, and chronicler of the adventures of, the famous detective Mr. Sherlock Holmes, has most mystifyingly disappeared without a trace. Foremost among the thoughts of the absent man's family and friends, of course, is terror lest he might have fallen into the hands of some criminal enemy of Mr. Sherlock Holmes, to be used as a pawn in some nefarious scheme, bandied as a hostage, or dispatched for the sake of revenge. Alternatively, concern has been expressed that, carrying his black bag identifying him as a physician, he might have been attacked by an anti-vaccination mob in the East End. No form of foul play at this time may be ruled out. Attempts are being made to trace Dr. Watson's movements this Wednesday last, on which day he departed to perform customary calls and errands but failed to return to his home and business in the evening. Cab-drivers are being questioned . . .

And so forth, a great many words to describe, essentially, nothing. An absence not newsworthy at all if it were not that my brother's name could be deployed in the headline. Dr. Watson had kissed his wife good-bye on Wednesday morning; this was Friday afternoon—the good doctor had been gone for two days. I imagined the police were saying, with some justification, that any number of harmless events might have caused the doctor's absence, and at any moment a telegram or letter should arrive explaining where and why he had been detained. "Attempts are being made" meant that the police were not yet investigating; otherwise the newspaper would have named the inspector in charge. No, at this point the only people really trying to locate Dr. Watson were two: his wife and his friend, my brother Sherlock Holmes.

And now one more: me.

But wait. What if Watson's absence had been arranged by my brother as a scheme to entrap me?

Sherlock knew that I had embroiled myself in two cases of missing persons. And while he might not understand that I had invented Dr. Leslie Ragostin, Scientific Perditorian, quite possibly he knew I had worked for the man. Did he appreciate that this was my life's calling, to be a finder of the lost?

Did he guess how very fond I was of the fatherly Dr. Watson?

Should I not, then, regard recent developments with the utmost suspicion?

But even as these eminently sensible considerations traversed my mind, already I was throwing the newspaper on the fire, then rummaging in my wardrobe, considering possible ways to disguise myself, possible strategies to find out the details of Dr. Watson's disappearance, how best to approach the matter. Indeed, a straitjacket could not have stopped me.

Although I knew I would have to be very careful.

Which presented some difficulty. Having spent the better part of the past month closeted in my lodging, bitter over my mother's failure to help me in my time of need—having been, in other words, idle and sulking—I now found myself woefully unprepared for action. There were a dozen items I required but did not have.

Wrapping a nondescript shawl around my head and shoulders, I sallied forth to acquire them. Mrs. Tupper would be pleased; I was going for a walk.

I did walk, all the way, because my emotions felt as tangled as the labyrinthine passages of the slums, my thoughts as

15

crowded and confused as the smutty tenements with their peaked garrets looming over me, and a long walk would perhaps help me compose my mind into some form of order.

My surroundings, however, did not promote serenity. A pieman cried, "'Ot meat tarts, two fer a penny!" while street urchins capered around him, mocking, "Puppies and kittens! Cats and rats!" meaning the probable meats in his pies, and a constable came frowning along to rout the lot of them for blocking traffic. While the day was indeed "springish," as Mrs. Tupper had said, the warming weather had increased the stench of the tenement privies—each of which served perhaps two hundred of London's Great Unwashed—and of the nearby Thames, and of the gas-works looming over the slums like a bloated shining caterpillar on steel legs, blighting everything beneath it.

Very well, I was perhaps failing to appreciate the beauty of the sunny day—a rarity in London, where clouds of smoke generally held sway no matter what the weather elsewhere—but truly, a hint of spring seemed only to increase the din and danger in the streets. I saw a district nurse in her old-fashioned black bonnet, long coat and white apron trying to make her way into a narrow court crisscrossed with clothes-lines of washing, while lounging men and street brats and even some women shouted curses, throwing mud and stones and horse droppings at her.

Brave woman, I thought, but I admit that my next consideration, as I walked on, was whether a nurse's garb might serve as a good disguise. Or perhaps the military-style black skirt and red jersey of one of General Booth's Hallelujah

Lassies? It seemed to me that people encountering someone in uniform observed the clothing, not the individual.

But Sherlock Holmes was no ordinary observer. Aware that I had masqueraded as a nun, he would be on the lookout for something else of the sort—a deaconess, a nanny, a nurse. No, I had to invent some disguise he could not possibly expect of me.

By now, blessedly, I had left the East End behind me. Instead of threading my way between tenements, I now walked pavements along wider, cobbled streets, and ahead of me loomed the dome of St. Paul's, a Grecian-columned landmark that contrasted strangely, I thought, with the shiny steel gas-works just as tall, not to speak of the gargoyled Gothic steeples of other churches nearby. Or the square-towered, corniced Italianate residence I was just then passing. Most of London was such a hodgepodge, railways and factories but also edifices French Second Empire and Moorish and Georgian and Regency, plus Tudor revival, or classical, revival this and revival that. A city uncertain, like me, of what appearance to present.

Here, even more so than in the East End, one saw all sorts of people. Well-dressed ladies shopped at the haberdashers and milliners and perfumeries, moving briskly about their business so that they would not be mistaken for much-adorned "ladies" of a different sort loitering on the pavements. Shop-girls mounted with the agility of goats to the tops of omnibuses, while visitors from the country gawked at everything: delivery boys on bicycles, bandbox-vendors with their wares on poles across their shoulders, chimney-sweeps trudging along as black as their brushes, ink-stained students carrying books, street musicians, gentlemen dressed in sober grey or black from head to toe, and "gents"—quite a different breed, "swell" dressers in search of amusement. My brothers had once hypothesised that I was masquerading as one of those.

Here came a short-haired woman in a billycock hat with a coachman cape, a stick in one gloveless hand, the leash of a bull terrier in the other—I am certain my brothers were afraid I was going to turn out even worse, perhaps puffing a cigar.

By now I was walking in the City itself, that is to say, the oldest part of London—one would think, London's centre, but it was not so, not any more than the Tower was London's centre, or Covent Garden, Piccadilly Circus or Trafalgar Square, or Buckingham Palace, or Westminster where the Houses of Parliament were. London had no more centre than one of Mrs. Tupper's sheep's-head stews did.

Resisting any further comparison between the city's confusion and my own current state of mind, I made my way towards Holywell Street.

A narrow, winding, dirty thoroughfare that could not have been more ironically misnamed or misused, its picturesque, high-gabled old buildings were given over mostly to vendors of low publications and cheap photographic prints. However, I was not here to look at lithographs of young ladies exposing their petticoats and legs whilst lacing their Balmoral boots. I sought a vendor of a different sort. As far back as the time of Queen Elizabeth, Holywell Street had housed mercers, and echoes of that silk-and-fancy-textile trade lingered on in the form of dealers in costume, finery, queer old clothing and the like, for masquerades. Wooden signs carved in the shape of masks grinned or grimaced down upon me most unpleasantly as I shouldered and elbowed my way through the crowded lane. Not only was Holywell Street itself quite ancient, crooked and narrow, but the print vendors' tawdry wares overflowed their shops onto the pavements, reaching out for one. Indeed, as I struggled along, a winsome little girl no more than six years old plucked at my sleeve, offering to sell me what appeared at first glance to be a pack of playing-cards. My second glance made me shudder and hasten onwards.

There. At last I saw, suspended from the overhanging eaves of a venerable lath-and-plaster building, a wooden sign which had likely been there as long as the structure itself. Carved in the shape of a cockerel, it had to mark the shop for which I was searching.

CHAPTER
THE
THIRD

I HAD FOUND OUT ABOUT IT during an adventure worth mentioning. A few weeks earlier, you see, my brother Sherlock had very nearly caught me. But in the crucial few minutes while he was summoning the constabulary to scour the streets for me, I had found an unlikely refuge: 221b Baker Street, that is to say, Sherlock's own lodgings, which I had entered by means of a plane-tree, a rooftop and a bedchamber window.

Ever since, I had wondered how my brother had reacted when, returning to his rooms at dawn, he had discovered my burnt cast-off nun's habit in his grate and a few items missing from his wardrobe. I imagined he had felt utterly chagrinned. Oddly, this thought did not make me smile.

Now, if it had been Mycroft . . .

Some other time, perhaps. As I was saying, hiding for several hours in Sherlock's lodging while he hunted me throughout every lane and alley, mews and court in the area,

I had put the time to good use by examining my brother's possessions. That man had an entire cabinet full of wigs and false beards and so on, but also accoutrements of disguise utterly new to me: face putty, stick-on warts and scars, dreadful (like ruined mediaeval battlements steeped in creosote) false teeth to cover his own well-kept ones, skull-caps to make him look bald or partly so, skin pigments varying from ruddy to swarthy, various false fingernails (unkempt, or yellow, or ridged, or overlong as if in mourning), a glue-on device to change the shape of his mouth and give him the look of a harelip—altogether, my eyes were opened. Wide. Where had my brother acquired such uncommonly useful items?

Searching his desk, then, I had found receipts from various shops, most of them in the theatre district and frankly intended to serve the needs of the stage—I hardly thought I could pass as an actress. But a few items several years ago had come from a shop in Holywell Street. A shop called Chaunticleer's.

So I thought I would try there first. My brother had not purchased anything at Chaunticleer's in some time; perhaps the place had closed? But there was only one way to find out, and if the shop remained, excellent: My brother had taken his business elsewhere for whatever reasons, and I would be unlikely to encounter him.

Chaunticleer's: hence the sign carved in the shape of a cockerel. *Chaunticleer* meant a cockerel, just as *Reynard* meant a fox. Where the latter had come from I had no idea, but the former I had read in one of Chaucer's *Canterbury Tales*.

Struggling across the teeming street—Holywell *always* thronged with all manner of Londoners ogling the pictures in the windows of the print-shops—I elbowed my way towards my destination.

Or was it my destination after all? Standing under the wooden cockerel—which had probably hung there since Shakespeare's day—to catch my breath before entering, I saw that the red lettering painted over the open door read, simply and mysteriously, Pertelote's.

Most peculiar.

I went in to see what was what.

Proceeding cautiously, I cast my glance anxiously about me, but neither of my brothers pounced from the shadows to seize me; indeed, the shop seemed empty. Racks of sheet music flanked the doorway, some used books had collected in a corner, and the bins and counters displayed an interesting variety of wares. Items for parlour amusements, I decided as I scanned them: cards of various sorts (though not, I am glad to say, of the tawdry sort I had been offered on the street), sets of dominoes, peg-board games, brightly coloured pick-up sticks, little play-scripts, stereopticons with story-photographs, a terribly clever miniature printing kit with moveable type and an inked pad . . . I was thoughtfully examining this last item when a contralto voice asked, "May I 'elp you?"

Looking up, I found myself facing a smiling woman of middle age who wore, along with a simple blouse and skirt, a comfortable yet unmistakable proprietorial air. This was *her* shop.

Even so, it took a moment for my rather overstrained mind to remember that Pertelote was the name of the practical-minded hen in Chaucer's Chaunticleer story.

No wonder Sherlock Holmes had stopped coming here. Somehow ownership had passed from cockerel to hen, so to speak, and—as our old butler's wife had once told me— neither of my brothers ever could abide a strong-minded woman.

"Um, Mrs. Pertelote?" I inquired.

Her smile warmed and widened as if at a private joke. "Per-*tell*-oh-tee," she said, correcting my pronunciation so cordially that I felt as though I had been complimented for my attempt. A large-boned woman, with a face like a platter and not a pretty one either, she wore her greying hair combed flat, then wound into two buns, one over each meaty, pendulous earlobe.

"What became of Chaunticleer?" I answered her smile, willing to share her amusement.

"Oh, 'e met 'is better."

"Yet you keep the carved cockerel sign?"

"Well, it's very old, and one must take care of old things, mustn't one." Her smile broadened, yet I felt the topic dismissed. "'Ow may I be of assistance?"

Even though she dropped "'er aitches," her accent was not entirely Cockney, but pleasantly semi-cultured. I tried to keep mine much the same as we conversed. Indicating the miniature, portable printing kit, I asked, "Could one make calling-cards with this?"

She did not blink, did not seem to wonder why such a

poorly clad woman would want any calling-cards, much less wish to print her own; she did not hesitate at all before answering, "Yes, indeed, but of a rather crude sort. I could make better ones for you, in the back room, if you just need a few."

"Indeed." I nodded. "Thank you. Might I look around your shop?"

"Certainly."

There were in fact many fascinating trifles and oddities for me to peruse—square wooden puzzles with tiles that could not be lifted out but slid within the frame, "talking boards" with numbers and letters for spiritualist experiments, velvet roses, music boxes, feather fans, silk scarves, vizard masks, some quite excellent quality wigs of long hair most likely shorn from fever victims, or possibly female convicts—but I took the time mainly because I needed to think. I wanted to accept Pertelote's offer to make me a few calling-cards—I foresaw needing at least one quite soon—but in order to have her print them, I must settle on an alias for myself.

Regarding which, my musings resumed where they had left off: *Ever me*, Everme? No. *Ever I*, Everi? Even worse. *Ever so*, Everso? Given a French twist, Everseau?

Not bad.

Very well; perhaps I would not have to use it for long. But what of a first name? Violet? No, a flower name—too risky. Viola? More evocative of a musical instrument than of a flower; Viola would do.

If the shop-owner were greedy, I ruminated, she could have sold me the miniature printing press for far more money

24

than she would make herself by printing a few cards for me on, apparently, a better press that she owned.

Hence, I found myself inclined to trust her, even though Pertelote was almost certainly not her real name. No matter. She was not to know my real name either.

In addition to the calling-cards, might I safely buy some even more compromising items from her?

I found myself inclined to think so.

But what if I were mistaken about her? What if she were the sort to talk?

It hardly mattered, for neither Mycroft nor Sherlock was likely ever to speak with her. Either one of them would shudder to go near such a woman, plainly in possession of herself, her own business and her own affairs.

Neither of my brothers could accept or understand a woman unattached to some man as wife, daughter or sister.

Both of them dismissed women as beyond the comprehension of logical thought. Neither of them could imaginatively enter the mind of any woman.

Much less mine. When I, a beak-nosed beanpole of a girl, had run away, I am sure that they had quite expected to find me disguised as a boy; to their way of thinking, how else could such an unfortunately plain female possibly manage?

But now they knew that I had masqueraded as a widow, and later as a nun, so probably they were on the lookout for another variation on the ugly-as-a-crow theme: a sharp-faced, veiled spinster perhaps? Or a scowling "platform woman" attempting to reform the slums? Probably they had stopped looking for me in male guise. So perhaps now it was time for me to adopt trousers?

No.

I simply did not want to. But more important, I had decided that, in order to find out the details concerning the disappearance of Dr. Watson, I would call upon Mrs. Watson, and in order to do that, I needed to be a woman.

But not such a woman as my brothers would ever suspect or even dream I could be.

Indeed—although I knew the undertaking would involve a tremendous amount of work—I would disguise myself in the last way that either Sherlock or Mycroft could possibly ever envision.

I would be beautiful.

CHAPTER
THE
FOURTH

I *WOULD* BE BEAUTIFUL.

This was, I admit, a decision prompted partly by spleen, bitterness of spirit caused by my mother but deflected onto the more acceptable target of Men; I had too often observed how men treated women, plain versus pretty. I planned to embark upon a kind of angry experiment: I would prove that these almighty males could be fooled.

But this was also a practical decision, for if I was walking into a trap—I could not yet dismiss the possibility that my brother and Watson had concocted an elaborate scheme to take me in—if it were so, why, I must walk out again unrecognised.

Even if the crisis were genuine (as I was more inclined to believe), then Mrs. Watson was sure to be in close touch with Sherlock Holmes, and if she were to mention to him that a tall, thin, ill-favoured girl with a pronounced nose and chin had come calling, he would certainly suspect it was me, and he would be on my trail like a bloodhound. If, however, Mrs. Watson were to mention a visitor of unusual comeliness, he would pay no attention whatsoever.

There was only one drawback to being beautiful: I wanted Mrs. Watson to confide in me, but women, even those who are themselves pretty, often dislike an attractive woman. And while unacquainted with Mrs. Watson personally, I knew she herself was unexceptional in appearance, having read in Dr. Watson's excellent account, *The Sign of the Four*, how he had met Mary Morstan (as she was then called) when she had consulted Mr. Sherlock Holmes. Watson had described his wife-to-be as having "neither regularity of feature nor beauty of complexion," but went on to say that "her expression was sweet and amiable, and her large blue eyes were singularly spiritual and sympathetic."

Perhaps, being good-natured, she would not after all resent me.

Also from *The Sign of the Four* I had learned that Mrs. Watson possessed "no relatives in England"—hence her visit to Holmes when she had found herself in perplexity. Her mother and father were dead. After boarding school, she had been a governess—not exactly a servant, but hardly on an equal standing with her employers either; most governesses dined alone. And alone, I suspected, was how she might find herself even now, for as a physician's wife, she remained in a position halfway between working class and gentry. If she had "led a retired life," having no circle of friends before her marriage, was she likely to have one since? I judged not. Poor folk who were in trouble ran straight to Mary, according to Dr. Watson—doubtless she shared his kindness of heart—but in her own time of trouble, would those same poor folk comfort her? I doubted it.

Some people wish to be alone in times of trial, but others craved company. While I had no way of knowing, I must take a chance that Mrs. Watson might be one of the latter, and might very much welcome the diversion of a visitor, even a stranger, at this difficult time.

I hoped so. Indeed, I hoped she would tell me something, however trivial, that would help me enlighten the mystery of her missing husband.

A truly lovely creature descended from a cab in front of Dr. Watson's office/residence the next afternoon—lovely with an innocent, modest, timeless beauty so artless that she wafted up the scrubbed white steps like a breath of fresh woodland air—

"Artless"? Hah. Hardly. Hours and hours of work had gone into the preparation of Miss Viola Everseau, and I could never have achieved such artlessness if it were not that the blood of artists runs in my veins. "Natural" beauty is all a matter of illusion, you see, an arrangement of proportions to foster a conspiracy of admiration amongst the senses of the beholder.

My brother Sherlock had once mentioned something of the sort. "Mycroft," he had said to my other brother, "the girl's head, you'll observe, is quite small in proportion to her remarkably tall body." He had been negatively assessing my intelligence at the time, and his conclusion was mistaken. But his statement itself was quite true.

Therefore I had purchased, at Pertelote's, a wig of exceptional luxuriance.

"Arrangement of proportions" in the case of feminine pulchritude means, first and foremost, arrangement of hair. And my own hair, even if it were not the colour of mud and the consistency of a marsh, is annoyingly located atop my head, where I cannot possibly see it or reach it properly to address it. But the wig! What a difference. I simply set it upon a candlestick in front of me, then arranged its shining rosewood-hued tresses until I got them exactly the way I wanted them, ringlets in a careless chignon at the crown, leaving a generous fringe around the forward edges.

Without the wig—and without the inserts I used to round out my cheeks and nostrils—I was a sharp-faced, hawk-nosed, sallow-skinned female version of my brother Sherlock.

But lovely and convincingly natural-looking hair so amended the proportions of my head that my pronounced nose and chin miraculously transformed into a classical Grecian profile. Framed by russet fringe and tresses, my skin looked not pallid, but delicately porcelain. Even I could scarcely believe the transformation.

There was more, much more, to be done, of course. Natural beauty requires a flaw, a certain wanton violation of symmetry, so I glued a small, raised port-wine birthmark (courtesy of Pertelote's) at my right temple, where it served to draw attention away from the center of my face—that is to say, my proboscis. I then dusted my face with rice powder as if attempting to hide the slight blemish. The rice powder was permissible for a lady to use, but the next item I took in hand, rouge, was not; I had to apply the disreputable substance very subtly to my cheekbones and lips. Then I had "Spanish papers" with which to rub my eyelids, making my eyes appear large and lustrous, but not so much that the artifice could be detected—it took me many attempts to get them right. As I have said, becoming beautiful required hours and hours of labour.

With, might I add, no guarantee at all that Mrs. Watson would receive me! It was quite possible that, under the circumstances, she had taken to her bed in nervous prostration, unable to entertain visitors even if she were willing.

Stars and garters! What if I were turned away from her door after all this work?

But one could but try. And at last, I was ready.

Taking a final look in the mirror, I must say I felt an unexpectedly fierce sensation of triumph.

Mrs. Tupper, unfortunately happening to see me going out, dropped the china pitcher she was carrying; it smashed to bits.

On that percussive note I took my cab to the Watson address, and if I wafted up the steps like a woodland breeze, it was because of my "Sylvan Paradise" eau de toilette, also purchased the day before. I had never in my life bothered with fragrance—let the gutters stink all they liked, I was never one to hold a scented handkerchief to my nose—but beauty, as I have said, lies not only in the eyes of the beholder, but in a carefully orchestrated conspiracy of all the senses. Hence, perfume. And I had swallowed honey to sweeten my voice. Corseting myself, I had made doubly sure that my bust enhancer remained free of lumps from any of the various objects I stored therein. Also, I had chosen my dress, as you might imagine, with great care, to appear neither humble nor aristocratic. Every "artless" thing about me, from my Gypsy bonnet—a small, flat hat with a few flowers—to my polished button-top boots, was the result of hours of trial and deliberation. Indeed, I had been up half the night preparing for this encounter. I could only hope that my sleeplessness gave soulful depth to the expression of my eyes.

And at the moment I reached my destination, of course, doubt swept in. What if I were a fool? What if the whole world could see that I was merely a crow masquerading as a peacock?

Just at that wretched moment, naturally, the door opened. But the bouquet I carried, snowdrops and jasmine (hope and sympathy) carefully arranged and bound by a yellow ribbon, explained my presence; there was no need for me to speak. I hoped that the parlour-maid did not notice how my gloved hand trembled as I laid my calling-card, *Miss Viola Everseau*, on her silver tray.

CHAPTER
THE
FIFTH

THE MAID SHOWED ME INTO A very modest parlour, then whisked away towards the back of the house to find her mistress. I stood looking around me. Each parlour window had been raised exactly two inches. Fortunately, in this part of London, the spring air stank only of smoke and street muck, odours mostly offset by the fragrance of the flowers I carried. In London, I had come to realise, those with any spare income at all considered flowers not a luxury, but a necessity for their homes and persons, in order to make living bearable to the sense of smell.

From the back of the house I heard a soft voice ask, "Who is it, Rose?" and then, without waiting for an answer, with my card still in her hand, Mrs. Watson entered the parlour, her face very pale yet composed. With quiet but warm concern she asked, "Have you come to see the doctor? I'm afraid he's not in. Is there anything I can do for you?"

I stood astonished, for I could see how red and swollen her eyes were. No longer could I doubt in the slightest that Dr. Watson indeed had disappeared, for Mrs. Watson's distress was genuine and evident. Yet she expected to render service, not to receive sympathy.

This amazing woman shamed me so much that, handing her the simple bouquet I had brought with me, I could barely speak coherently. "I read about it in the news," I babbled, "and I cannot imagine why, for he's so very kind, your husband I mean, I do hope he is all right, I beg your pardon for intruding at such a difficult time, but I thought perhaps some flowers—"

Other bouquets had arrived, I saw, but not so many as to crowd the small parlour.

"How very thoughtful of you. Thank you." Mrs. Watson's lip trembled as she accepted the snowdrops and jasmine from me, but her gentle gaze upon my face remained inquiring.

"I have been a patient of your husband's," I added hastily in reply to her unspoken request that I should please explain myself, as I should have done in the beginning.

She nodded, humbly accepting the presence of a very young, rather bird-brained, and quite attractive (I hoped) stranger in her parlour. "You'll forgive me, I'm sure. I do not know all of his patients."

"You can hardly be expected to! And when I saw, in the paper, you know—well, I just had to do something, for he not only remedied my difficulty, but showed the greatest tact and sympathy in doing so." This was true, in a way. When lying, I always make every possible use of the truth;

I can carry it off better that way, and remember more easily what I have said.

"But how thoughtful of you—what a lovely gesture—your being here."

Feeling painfully like a fraud, I mentally reminded myself quite sternly that I *was* here to help her.

"What lovely flowers," she continued, cradling them in one arm as if holding a baby. "Miss Everseau, I'd be most obliged—I mean, if it is no inconvenience—would you care to stay awhile and have some tea?"

It was as I had thought it might be: No matter what her natural reserve, at this time of trouble Mrs. Watson needed someone, any safe and sympathetic listener, to talk to. As soon as we were seated, with only the slightest encouragement from me she began to tell me how her husband had left the house in excellent humour this past Wednesday morning, planning to make some house calls then perhaps stop at his club—but in the evening he had not returned.

"I kept his supper warm till it turned to cinder," she said in a sort of bewilderment, "and still I could not bring myself to throw it into the dustbin, because to do so would have been to acknowledge that he was terribly overdue, and I could not yet admit that anything—something—had happened. I kept telling myself he would be home any minute. He had to be."

She had waited all night for him, and in the morning she had sent for the police and, of course, for Sherlock Holmes. (She assumed, correctly, that I understood her husband's association with the famous detective.) The police had arrived first but refused to take action until they saw evidence of a crime.

"They said wait a bit, it's not uncommon for a man to disappear for a day or two or three, then come home all sheep-faced, having spent the time drunk or in an opium den or with some loose woman."

"Did they actually *say* that?" I exclaimed.

"Not in so many words, but one could tell well enough what they meant. As if John would ever do any such thing." Even in the heat of righteous indignation Mrs. Watson's tone remained sweet. "Luckily, Mr. Sherlock Holmes came soon after, and set about finding out what had happened."

"And has he done so?"

"He said I would not hear from him until he had something to report, and I have not."

"Has he no theory?"

"He wonders whether some villain is attempting revenge against him, of course. John himself has no enemies."

"No disagreeable patients?"

"Well, of course there is always that. Mr. Holmes took John's medical record-books to check."

Good. Then she herself was unlikely to look up Viola Everseau in them.

I leaned towards her. "Mrs. Watson, what do *you* think has happened?"

For a moment her composure faltered. She had to lift her hands to her face. "I truly cannot imagine."

Just then the maid brought in the tea-tray. Making a visible effort, Mrs. Watson rallied and, as she poured, changed the subject. "Do you live with your family here in London, Miss, ah, Everseau?"

I told her that no, I lived alone, had worked in an office, was without employment just now and hoped to find a position in Fleet Street. All true—not that it mattered; if I had told her I rode bareback in a circus, she would have nodded just the same, for her distress was such that she could comprehend nothing.

We sipped tea in awkward silence.

For something to say, I complimented the room in which we sat. "Such lovely lithographs. I quite approve of the combination of comfortable furnishings with touches of culture."

I quite approved of Mrs. Watson herself, actually, so bravely serving a second cup of tea while she looked around her own parlour as if she had never been there before.

I added, "What a lovely little spinnet." Having been a governess, of course she had spent half her life at the keyboard of a piano, but I asked anyway, "Do you play?"

She scarcely heard the question, of course, poor thing. "Oh, um, yes. Yes, I . . ." Her sorely preoccupied thoughts wandered, apparently, to a posy of daisies placed upon the instrument. "So many flowers do serve to console one," she remarked vaguely. "Somewhat, at least. And from strangers, yet. People are so kind."

Nodding agreement, I privately thought she was rejoicing over crumbs, for there were not many flowers at all. There was of course the bouquet I had brought—which, I was glad to see, the maid had placed in a vase exactly as I had arranged it.

Apart from that, there was a little nosegay of lily-of-the-valley, wishing Mrs. Watson the return of happiness, there were the ubiquitous carnations, some white roses, and—

And tucked away on a corner table, the most bizarre bouquet I had ever seen in my life.

I am sure I sat up straighter, and my eyes widened, but I kept myself from saying anything more than a murmured "How peculiar!"

"What?" Slowly Mrs. Watson turned to see what had caught my attention. "Oh. Yes, odd, isn't it? The poppies should be red, but they're white, and the may should be white, but it's red, and I have no idea what the greens are."

"Asparagus!" I marvelled. Not the vegetable, of course, but the cobwebby fronds that spring up afterwards, with leaves like sparse grey-green hair. "Once it's grown, you know." Which it should not be, at this time of year; only the spears should be sprouting from the ground.

Mrs. Watson blinked. "My goodness, how clever you are! How did you learn that?"

"My mother was a botanist." True enough, and it might have been said of half the genteel ladies in England; flowers and botany were considered to be a female hobby.

"And she studied asparagus? I've never seen it placed in a bouquet before."

"Neither have I." But if the greens were bizarre, the blossoms were worse; their significance chilled me.

Taking care not to reveal this in the tone of my voice, I asked, "Mrs. Watson, are you familiar with what is sometimes called the language of flowers?"

"Only a little. There has been small occasion for such communication in my life." She said this with gentle good humour. "The may signifies hope, does it not, and the poppy, comfort?"

"In the French tradition, yes." But this was England, and in British folklore, hawthorn—what she called "may"— was a shrub long associated with pagan deities and with faeries, a powerful symbol of bad luck. No countrywoman would ever bring a sprig of its pretty cluster blossoms indoors, for to do so might bring down calamity upon the house, even death.

I did not say this. But I did say, "The red poppy implies comfort, I believe, but the white poppy symbolises sleep."

"Really?" She thought about that for a moment, then actually smiled. "Well, I certainly could do with some sleep."

"What a very odd bouquet. Who, might I ask, gave it to you?"

"Why, I don't know. I believe a boy brought it to the door."

Setting my cup of tea aside, I stood, crossing the room to have a better look. The poppies must have been forced in a hothouse—all flowers except snowdrops came from hothouses at this time of year; nothing remarkable in that. But that the *asparagus* should have been so cultivated—most peculiar. Explicable, perhaps, if someone had a boundless yearning for the vegetable—but the hawthorn? Who on earth would trouble with such a useless prickle-bush as hawthorn in a hothouse, when like a weed it grew everywhere in the countryside?

39

Upon studying the hawthorn more closely, I saw that its jagged branches were wound round with tendrils of a delicate vine whose white flowers had already wilted.

Bindweed.

A sort of wild trumpet-flower, bindweed would be as common as sparrows in country hedgerows come summertime. But like the hawthorn, this early in the year, it must have been forced indoors. More, it must have been cultivated *with* the hawthorn, to entwine it so.

Bindweed? More correctly known as convolvulus, the plant indicated something convoluted—something stealthy, entangling, twisted.

And this ominous bouquet, it seemed to me, had come from quite a twisted mind. I had to find out—

But as I turned to question Mrs. Watson in more detail, the parlour door burst open and, without waiting for the maid to announce him, a tall, impeccably clad yet vehement gentleman strode in, almost swooped in, his manner as hawk-like as the keen profile of his face: Mr. Sherlock Holmes.

CHAPTER
THE
SIXTH

I REGRET TO SAY THAT I GASPED aloud, both in terror and in admiration—those two emotions seem always to attend my dealings with my renowned brother. To me his craggy features were the most handsome in England, his grey eyes the most brilliant, and if circumstances were different . . . but there was no time for pointless dreams. I fully comprehended all the peril of my situation, and I admit that I felt a strong inclination to flee. Luckily, in contemplation of the bizarre bouquet I stood so near the wall that it checked my impulse to back away. Had I made such an ill-considered move, I am sure my brother might have noticed.

But he barely glanced at me, although it took me several thudding heartbeats to comprehend why, for there I stood in plain sight, his tall, gawky, long-nosed sister Enola—until I realised that my disguise had kept him from really looking at me. Indeed, the moment he saw a winsomely coifed and attired young woman in the parlour along with Mrs. Watson, he turned his attention elsewhere. One might think he disliked to be in company with such a woman.

And he did not hear my gasp, for at the same time Mrs. Watson jumped up with a cry. "Mr. Holmes!" She stretched both hands towards him. "Have you—is there—any news of John?"

To judge by his taut and sombre face, not any good news. As if capturing two fluttering doves he took Mrs. Watson's hands in his kid-gloved grasp, but he did not speak, only made a shushing motion with his lips and threw a warning glance in my direction.

"Oh! How thoughtless of me!" Hardly what he meant to convey; he wanted her to get rid of me, but she seemed to feel that she had been rude, forgetting to introduce me. Freeing her hands, she turned to me. "Miss, um . . ."

If one is literally trembling with ill-mixed emotion, one might as well make the best use of it. Relieving Mrs. Watson of the necessity of remembering my name, I squealed, "Is this *really* Mr. Holmes, the great detective?" Simulating great girlish excitement, I hurried forward, smiling, nay, grinning like a skull. "Oh, I am so thrilled!" I squeaked, my voice a full octave above its usual level. Even as I quaked in fear that my brother might recognise me, I grasped one of his gloved hands in both of mine. "Oh, just wait until I tell my aunt that I met the famous Mr. Sherlock Holmes!"

My effusions had the effect I desired: If a sewer rat had crawled upon Sherlock it might have repulsed him less. He could not bear to look me in the face, turning his head away as he said frostily, "Miss, ah . . ."

"Everseau. Miss Viola Everseau," I burbled.

"Miss Everseau, will you kindly excuse us?"

"Of *course*. Absolutely. I know you and Mrs. Watson—that is, you have important matters to discuss—I am frightfully honoured and delighted to have met you—" Twittering inanities, I allowed myself to be ushered away by the faithful parlour-maid Rose, who had appeared for that purpose with my wrap in her hands.

Even after I heard the front door of the Watson residence close behind me, I could not quite believe my escape. Mincing down the stone steps, I expected at any moment to hear Sherlock shout, "Wait a moment! Enola? Enola! Constable, stop that girl in the wig!"

But instead I heard his voice speaking to Mrs. Watson: "There is no very good news, I am afraid." The words, although quietly and gravely spoken, carried clearly to me through the partially opened parlour windows. "But I have found something. I have found Watson's medical bag."

I stopped on the pavement where I stood. Oh. Oh, my goodness, I couldn't simply leave; the sound of my brother's voice acted upon me like a magnet upon needles and pins. I had to know more—but what if I were caught listening?

Pretending to search my pockets for something, I glanced up and down the street, which lay quiet except for a milkmaid making her deliveries and a cab or two. London is odd that way; slum streets brawl always with women standing in open doorways shouting at one another, children running amok

43

in the muck, beggars, vendors, drunkards, idlers—but the better residential streets lie almost empty. There, scrubbed doorsteps lead up to closed doors flanked by windows without a single broken pane of glass—instead, one sees potted geraniums, a canary in a hanging cage, a meek little "Room to Let" sign, lace curtains.

But one cannot tell whether one is being watched from behind the lace curtains.

Holmes spoke on. "I found it at his club, where someone had stowed it out of sight behind a davenport. It remained unnoticed until today."

"But . . . John would not have left . . ." Mrs. Watson's quiet voice struggled against tears.

"Exactly." My brother's voice also repressed strong emotion—my heart swelled when I heard such controlled anguish in his words. "No doctor, least of all Watson, would ever willingly be separated from his black bag."

Wary of my own feelings, I realised I was quite likely to betray myself with a whimper or some equally undignified involuntary utterance. *Enola, you silly chit*, I mentally scolded myself, *get away!*

I moved, however, only a few steps, just enough so that Holmes and Mrs. Watson would not see me if either of them happened to glance outside; I put myself on a line with the corner of the house and of the parlour. There I stood fiddling with my gloves while trying to calm my breathing and the pounding of my heart.

I could still hear my brother speaking. "Therefore, I think we can now rule out the possibility of accident. Watson was purposefully lured or spirited away by some person or agency unknown."

Mrs. Watson's soft reply was inaudible to me.

"I cannot be certain, but it seems to me that the anti-medical elements, yammering as if surgery were vivisection, tend towards hysteria and are unlikely to act with such organised decision. Yet, although improbable, it remains just possible, as do other hypotheses. Some enemy from Watson's army days, perhaps; I have been looking into that possibility, but my instincts tell me otherwise. Above all I continue to suspect the criminal underworld, but my informants so far have been able to tell me nothing. It is as if one moment Watson were playing billiards at his club, and the next, the earth opened up. "

With a tattoo of hooves on cobbles a delivery-van rattled past, the driver glancing at me curiously, probably wondering why I was standing there. In London, any unchaperoned woman who pauses even for a moment to blow her nose puts herself in danger of being taken for a "social evil," the polite term for a lady of the night.

"It is this silence, this hiatus, that I cannot understand," Sherlock was saying when the noise had passed. "If Watson was kidnapped, why no demand for ransom? If taken by some enemy, why no gloating message of revenge? We should have heard from such a tormenter by now. Have you anything to report? Anything at all out of the ordinary?"

Her reply was brief.

"Flowers?" said Holmes with dismissive impatience. "But surely such social gestures are to be expected. No, if we are to involve the police, we need something more than a black bag and an anonymous bouquet. Please think. Is there nothing—"

Mrs. Watson said something in broken tones.

"It is true, logic suggests no reason why murder might not have taken place." My brother's voice had tightened to the breaking point. "And in that case there would be no communication. Yes, I have thought it too. Yet I cannot give up hope. One must not give up hope! And," he added with black fire flaring in his tone, "I will not rest until I have got to the bottom of this affair."

A considerable silence followed, during which another vehicle trundled past, this time a brougham, the driver and occupants eyeing me askance. I felt like a target set up for marksmanship practice.

Finally my brother spoke again. "We must persevere; we cannot do otherwise. Can you think of nothing to help me?"

Silence.

"Have you had visitors? Other than that syrupy young woman who left just now? Who was she, by the way?"

Oh, my goodness. My nerves could take no more; I left, walking down the street in the manner recommended by *Ladies' Moral Companion*, "self-possessed and quietly, with not too much lagging and not too swift a step, looking as if one understands what one is about . . ." Only after I had rounded a corner did I let my breath out.

I wondered whether I had now been added to Sherlock's list of suspects.

I certainly hoped not. I did not want him interested in the "syrupy young woman." All the more so because he must not waste his time while trying to find out what had happened to Watson—

But he *was* wasting his time, I realised as I entered a crowded thoroughfare of shops and businesses. ("Avoid lounging about the shop-windows; resolutely forego even the most tempting displays of finery. Pass men without looking at them, yet all the while seeing them . . .") Brilliant as my brother was at unravelling many sorts of perplexities, he continued to err by neglecting the women's sphere: in this case, the messages conveyed by flowers.

It seemed to me that a gloating message of revenge had indeed arrived in the form of hawthorn, poppies, convolvulus, and the oddest of greens: asparagus.

The asparagus I did not at all understand. Nevertheless, I felt fairly sure that the bizarre bouquet had not come from the criminal underworld, nor from anyone Watson had known in the army. No, I thought, it had come from someone who would not last long in either of those organisations, someone too odd for them. Someone eccentric, petty and spiteful in quite a creative way, someone enjoying an interesting "garden" variety of gleeful madness. And someone so dedicated to the pursuit of botanical malice that he—or she—grew hawthorn in a hothouse.

CHAPTER
THE
SEVENTH

BUT HOW TO FIND THIS interesting person?

Three possible schemes came to mind, and while one (locate and investigate hothouses) would take too long, another seemed more hopeful. I immediately put it into action, finding a place to sit down and write.

As it was a fine day, I chose a bench near one of West London's new public drinking-water fountains, quite as big as most war memorials and surmounted by winged figures; halfway up its magnificence flared a basin intended, I think, to look like a scallop shell but more resembling a fungus jutting from a tree, with a porpoise-shaped spout giving forth refreshment for ladies and gentlemen. Lower down a similarly ornate trough was provided for the pleasure of horses, and lower yet, near the pavement, a smaller trough for the use of dogs and, I supposed, cats, rats and street urchins. Sitting, as I have said, where I could view the intermingled species enjoying this monument to benevolent hygiene,

I drew paper and pencil from a pocket and composed a message to be placed in the personal columns of all the London newspapers. After several attempts, I distilled it to greatest simplicity:

Hawthorn, convolvulus, asparagus and poppies: what do you want? Reply this column. M.M.W.

The initials stood for Mary Morstan Watson, as if the query had been posted by her.

Satisfied, I recopied this numerous times for London's plethora of publications. Then, by hopping onto a passing tram (which, as a modern urban woman, I had learned to do without stopping the horses), I paid my penny and was rewarded with a ride to, eventually, Fleet Street.

Many a time I had visited the Fleet Street offices of the various news publishers, and had been waited upon politely but indifferently by various male clerks. This time, however, while even more than usually polite, they seemed far from indifferent. Preoccupied as I was by concerns other than my appearance, I did not at first realise the reason for the change.

Oh, for goodness' sake! I fumed to myself when I remembered I was wearing a great deal of hair and lady-be-fair artifice. *What fools.*

After I had delivered and paid for all my advertisements, the day was turning to night and I was getting quite tired. But I could not yet rest, for I needed immediately to pursue my other scheme to identify the sender of the bizarre bouquet.

One does not cultivate hawthorn, twined with bindweed yet, in a hothouse just for a single triumphant moment; such a spiteful person, I believed, would continue to send his or her messages of hatred in floral form. And when the next one arrived, I wanted to be in a position to observe and intercept.

Therefore, I needed to return to the scene. So much the better that night had now fallen; darkness was to my advantage, lessening the likelihood that Mrs. Watson might see me as I reentered her street of residence. For additional concealment I hailed a cab.

I had the cab-driver pull up directly in front of my destination, and I had him wait, so that the cab—a big four-wheeler—stood between me and the residence of John Watson, M.D. The house with the "Room to Let" sign in the window, you see, stood almost directly across the street from the Watsons'.

Mentally I begged fate or fortune as I plied the door-knocker: Please, might the room in question have a window facing in that direction.

It did.

Perfect.

Perfect, I mean, in that one all-important aspect. In others it was dreadful—chill, bare and cheerless, with a bed as hard as a board and nearly as narrow, and a flinty-eyed, disagreeable landlady who named far too high a weekly cost. Small wonder the shrew's spare room had remained vacant until now. I haggled with her over rent and terms, but only for the sake of appearances; the truth was, I would have taken the room at whatever price, and ended up handing over my money and receiving my latch-key within a few minutes.

I needed to be in place by the following morning, you see. Already, during the half-day I had spent away, a second suspicious bouquet might have arrived at the Watsons' door—a most provoking thought. But even so, I felt no doubt that the malicious sender would eventually provide another, and when it arrived, I must not miss it.

So I had my cab-driver take me to Aldersgate, where I dismissed him and, after going in one door of the railway station and out the other, I engaged another cab. Such precautions had become second nature to me; I must never forget that cab-drivers can be questioned and that I was a fugitive, with the world's greatest detective taking quite a personal interest in me.

I had the other cab, then, take me to an East End street where few if any cabs had gone before: that is to say, to my lodging. And I had the driver wait while I packed the things I needed, meanwhile attempting to explain to a rather dismayed and doubtful Mrs. Tupper, "I am going to visit my aunt for a few days."

"Eh?" She lifted her hearing-trumpet to her ear.

"I am going to visit my aunt."

"Eh?" With her watery old eyes widened to their utmost, she still could not understand, yet would not venture nearer to me. Standing in the doorway of my room, watching a lovely young lady throw clothing into a holdall, knowing that for the past month a girl who more resembled a scarecrow had barely stirred from the room, I am sure she wondered whether I had gone mad, whether she ought to summon a constable to have me committed lest I constituted a threat to the body public. "Eh? Going where? At this time of night?"

"Going! Visit! Aunt!" I shouted into her ear-trumpet. With a satchel in each hand I whisked past her out the door.

The next morning—Sunday—found me applying rouge, birthmark, powder, et cetera, in order to face the day in lovely ladylike guise—quite a nuisance, this new disguise; all over London, women readying themselves for church were struggling less. But at least my wig did not yet need to be restyled; atop a bedpost—for I did not wish to put on the hot, heavy thing until necessary—it perched at the ready with its hat still pinned in place. So as not to be seen without it, I made the loathsome landlady bring my breakfast upstairs, leaving it on a tray outside my door. Meanwhile, corseted to simulate an hourglass figure and wearing quite a fetching puffed-and-pleated Paris-green day-dress, I sat in the window with a pair of opera glasses close at hand, watching the street in general and the Watson residence in particular while taking advantage of the concealing qualities of lace curtains.

As regarded concealment, only my precipitous arrival made it necessary. After a few days it wouldn't matter if Mrs. Watson saw me about; indeed, I might approach her and tell her how fortunate I had been to see the "Room to Let" sign on my previous visit just when I was looking for a new lodging-place, and was there any news of Dr. Watson?

On the other hand, I quite hoped this vigil would not last so long as a few days, for even within the first few hours it had become exquisitely boring. "Nice" streets were too quiet.

A scattered procession of cabs with Sunday licences, scrubbed and shining in order that cleanliness might actually contain godliness, brought various neighbours, including Mrs. Watson, home from worship.

Mrs. Watson, I noticed, took a few moments to pat the cab-horse; rare was the woman who would do that, especially at the risk of besmirching her Sunday best. I regarded Dr. Watson's winsome wife with mingled admiration and pity; she wore black, as if already she were in mourning.

After the churchgoers had gone indoors, nothing at all happened for an hour or so.

Eventually a bent old woman in a shawl limped from door to door, selling violets from a large flat basket.

That was all for the next half hour or thereabouts.

A water-wagon passed at a trot, the horse with tail handsomely lifted, pleasing to watch until one realised the nag was littering the length of the street with horse-apples. Ironic, as the purpose of the water-wagon was to clean London's streets, typically covered with muck a respectable slug would not have crawled in. The labour of clearing it could not pause even for Sunday rest, for there were a great many horses in the city, and each one produced forty-five pounds of waste per day, or so Mother had once told me—

Don't think of Mother.

To distract myself, I tugged at the tasteful opal brooch centered upon my dress front, thus drawing the slender dagger sheathed in the busk of my corset, the opal being its pommel. Hefting my weapon by its hilt, I felt reassured. I had used it once, on a garroter. Although once an attacker of a different sort had used a knife on me—but my corset had foiled his attempt to stab me. Thus convinced of the value of corsets, I had provided myself with several specially made so that their metal ribs did not nip my waist or jab me under the armpits, only protected me from the likes of Jack the Ripper, while supporting the bust enhancer and hip regulators which disguised my stick-like figure while serving as holdalls, containing emergency supplies plus a small fortune in Bank of England notes—courtesy of Mother.

Do not think about Mother!

Hastily slipping my dagger between the buttons on the front of my dress, returning it to its sheath in my bosom, I set myself to taking mental inventory of the other items therein. Bandaging, scissors, iodine, spare stockings, needle and thread—

In her best blue cape and bonnet a nanny walked past on the street below, pushing a parasol perambulator with one hand while with the other she led a toddler in a lacy pink dress and white pinafore.

Yawn.

—head-scarf, hair extensions, pince-nez spectacles for disguise, lorgnette by way of magnifying lens, smelling-salts, sweets, biscuits—

Around the far corner of the street appeared a small, ragged boy carrying a bunch of flowers nearly bigger than he was.

Inventory and ennui at once forgotten, I grabbed for my opera glasses and peered through them, trying to identify the blossoms in the bouquet. But the boy, confounded ignorant street urchin, carried it under his arm, head down, as if it were likely to bite him otherwise. I could hardly see the flowers at all, and had to content myself for the moment with memorising the boy's scruffy plaid clothing and rather stupid face. He paused with his mouth open to study each house number.

Very possibly he might not be looking for the Watson residence at all, might not concern me whatsoever.

My heart pounded in protest at the thought. *Nonsense. It has to be—*

It was.

After studying the number beside the door at inordinate length, he turned to ascend the steps of the Watson residence.

Only then, as he put his back to me, could I catch a clear look at the flowers in the bouquet.

Laburnum.

Harebells.

Convolvulus again.

Wispy sprays of *asparagus* again.

Sprigs of yew.

Ye gods.

Dropping the opera glasses, I sprang up, popped my wig (hat and all) onto my head, snatched my mantle and ran out of my temporary lodging and down the stairs, intent on catching that boy as soon as he had completed his delivery.

CHAPTER
THE
EIGHTH

LABURNUM, YOU SEE, WHILE A very pretty flower, hangs down in yellow cascades, "weeping."

The blue harebell, long associated with faeries, bad luck and fey events, means "submission to grief."

The yew is a graveyard tree, signifying death.

So even if it were not for the convolvulus and the asparagus fronds, I would have felt sure: These flowers came from the same spiteful source as that other bizarre bouquet, and might not this evil-minded person be responsible for the disappearance of Dr. Watson?

I scooted downstairs, out the front door and onto the street as quickly as possible, but only to find the confounded fish-mouthed boy—who had approached the Watson residence so very slowly—now trotting off at a goodly pace, just disappearing around the opposite corner.

Oh, no. No, he was not getting away from me. Snatching up the front of my skirt with both hands, I ran after him.

I am long of limb and love to run—I have always been the disgrace of my family, running, climbing, and generally acting like a biped—but that accursed skirt slowed me down even as I hoisted it to my knees, for doing so denied me the proper pumping action of my arms. Other parts of my personage compensated so that my head wobbled and I swayed from side to side, altogether, I am sure, resembling a tall Paris-green goose in a tremendous hurry.

Onlookers regarded me with shock. I remember speeding past a lady who stood like a pillar of salt with both silk-gloved hands to her gawking mouth, and as for gentlemen, how my display of my lower limbs affected them I can scarcely say, for, let a lady in an evening-gown show ever so much bosom, still not an inch of ankle must ever peep from beneath her skirt—but I did not care what I looked like or what anyone thought, for as I sprinted around the corner I spied the street urchin cavorting along not too far ahead of me.

"Boy!" I called to him.

Pleasantly enough, I thought, and I fully expected him to turn, and stop, and we would have a nice little talk, and I would give him a penny—but instead, he took one look at me over his shoulder, his lackwit eyes widened, and he tore off like a hare before the hounds.

The stupid little bounder, whatever was he frightened of?

"Boy! Nincompoop, wait! Come back here!" Without breaking stride I sped after him, gaining on him easily, stunted little slum-bred brat. I should have caught him within a moment if he had not made towards Covent

Garden and dodged into streets filled with traffic. Rather than keeping to the pavement, he took to the cobbles, dashing between potato-wagons and carts and cabs and almost under the hooves of coach-horses; here, being born and weaned in the city, he had a great advantage over a country girl who had never been much accustomed to ducking omnibuses! He led me a jolly good chase until finally I lost sight of him entirely.

Stopping at the corner where I had last seen him, I stood hot-faced and panting, one hand hauling up my skirt while with the other I disciplined my wig, which felt as if it were about to take leave of my head—confounded thing, no matter how annoying, I should have put it on beforehand and secured it with hairpins—too out of breath to mutter the naughty phrases that came to mind, I looked about me in every direction, with no idea which way to turn.

I nearly gave up. Actually, I did give up. With a sigh of exasperation and defeat I let my skirt—such parts of it as were not already sodden with horse muck—drop at last to decently cover my ankles. Then, ignoring the stares of dressed-to-be-seen Sunday strollers, I applied both hands to the problem of the slipping wig. Trying to restore some order to my appearance, I lifted it to straighten it—

"Don't!" screamed a high-pitched voice.

Startled, I looked for the source of this terrified plea and discovered the street urchin, the selfsame boy I had been chasing, staring at me huge-eyed from his hiding place inside one of the crates (meant for displaying dry goods) flanking the closed door of the corner chandler. Standing where I was, I had unknowingly blocked his escape, but I might never have seen him had he not cried out.

"No, please, don't!" he wailed.

I stood, immobilised by astonishment, with a hand at each side of my wig. "Don't *what*?" I blurted. I could not imagine what he was so afraid of.

He shrieked, "Don't take yer 'air off! Don't take yer nose off either!"

"*Oh,*" I said, nodding slowly and wisely, as if he had explained everything. Obviously the boy was a halfwit and needed to be approached cautiously. Taking care to make no sudden movements, as if faced with a cornered animal, I let my wig lapse back onto my head in whatever fashion it so desired. "All right," I added in easy, soothing tones. "No harm done. Would you like a penny?" Reaching into a pocket, I pulled out a handful of coins.

Hearing the jingling sound and catching sight of the shiny metal, the lad seemed to calm, or at least to shift the focus of his anxiety, as I had thought he might.

"I just want to talk with you a moment. Will you come out?" I coaxed.

"No!"

"Why, then, I'll come in, if you don't mind." I simply plopped myself down to sit on the pavement in front of the crate within which he cowered. Fatigue alone, I think, would not have made me do this—although I was indeed quite fagged from running—but I found the absurdity of the situation irresistible. All around me I heard horrified gasps arise from onlookers, and I sensed how they stepped

59

away, as if my extraordinary conduct might spread some sort of contagion. Just two years before, during the Queen's Golden Jubilee, a lady had sat down on one of the pathways within the Crystal Palace in order to place a sprig of fir into the top of her boot; not long afterwards she had been committed to a madhouse.

By her husband. Not uncommonly a woman might be put away in a lunatic asylum for insane conduct such as reading novels, going to spiritualist meetings, quarrelling, failure to obey, et cetera. Having one's wife taken off by "body snatchers" in a black barouche was a respectable recourse should her presence become onerous, whereas divorce was a scandal.

It was quite a good thing that I planned to have no husband, I thought, smiling and still panting from "running mad." Seated knee-to-knee with my quarry as if we were two children playing teatime, I told the filthy little street savage, "How do you do. I am very pleased to meet you." As if selecting a bonbon, I lifted a penny between my fingers. "I could not help observing your taking quite a lovely bouquet of flowers to the Watson residence just now."

Warily the boy countered, "Don't know no Watson," but his gaze had fixed on the copper coin.

"How did you know which house, then?"

"The man told me the number."

"What man?"

"Why, the man 'oo took off 'is nose."

My mind began to feel as fagged as my legs, but I only

60

nodded slowly and sagely once more, deciding to circumvent the nasal improbability for the time being. "And how did you happen to meet this man?"

"'E called me over." The lad demonstrated a beckoning gesture such as any person of any consequence might use to summon any boy loitering in the street if the latter was wanted to carry a parcel, take a message, hold a horse by the reins or render any simple service.

"Was he in a gig or a dog-cart?" I inquired.

"No! 'E were in a right shiny carriage, 'e were, wit' 'orses."

Refraining from telling him that a dog-cart was also a horse-drawn vehicle, I merely asked, "A phaeton? A brougham?"

"Don't know 'bout no broom. A fine black carriage it were, with yellow spokes to the wheels."

A description which could apply to half the vehicles in London. I tried again. "Did you see a coat-of-arms?"

"Sure, 'e had a coat on and harms too. Both harms, and 'ands. 'E give me the posy wit' one and tuppence wit' the other."

Losing his fear of me, the lad was becoming more loquacious—a good thing, as I found myself rather at a loss, trying to question this boy with a head too large for his stunted body and intelligence too small. "Um, what did this man look like?"

"Wot like? Wot's any toff like? Just a long-faced tove in chin-whiskers 'n a top-'at, except that 'e took 'is nose off."

There it was again.

"He took his nose off?" I strove to keep incredulity out of my tone.

Apparently I succeeded, or else the horror of the memory had taken such hold of the boy that he could not help but speak. All in a rush he said, "Knocked it off against the door, like, when 'e stuck 'is 'ead out t' give me the flowers. It fell on 'is lap, an' I don't know wot scared me worse, that nose lyin' there or the way 'e grabbed it and cursed me and shook it at me, tol' me take the flowers right smart or 'e'd come after me and do the same to me and pull out me eyes into the bargain."

"Um, did you see any blood?"

"No!" The lad started to tremble. "No more'n if 'is face wuz made of wax."

"What did he have where his nose should have been?"

"Nothin'! Wot I mean, 'e was just 'oles, like a skeleton." The boy shivered.

"Holes?"

But the lad had gone into a convulsive fit of shuddering. "Please, don't take yer 'air off or yer ears or nothin'!"

"Oh, for goodness' sake, why would I? Did the man put his nose back on?"

"I don't know! I ran! I took 'is flowers just as 'e said and then you come chasing me!" The street urchin started sobbing, not the usual forthright roar of a young barbarian, but a wail of soul-felt distress. His odd encounter, apparently, had upset him considerably. "What were ye chasing me fer?"

"Never mind." I rose to my feet (aware that each well-bred

person passing by gave me a long stare and a wide berth) and handed the child a sixpence instead of a penny, for I felt sorry to have caused him distress. Evidently there was no more sense to be got out of him.

Sense? What sense was there in anything I had learned?

CHAPTER
THE
NINTH

RETURNING AT ONCE TO my temporary lodgings by the most inconspicuous route, I rang for hot water. While I washed, put on a clean dress, sponged the skirt of the soiled one and tidied my hair—that is to say, took off my wig, combed it out, and pinned it up in an acceptably attractive fashion—I thought.

Or tried to think, but succeeded only in wondering how the man had lost his nose. I vaguely recalled that, sometime during the Renaissance, there had been a colourful Danish astronomer who had lost his in a duel, but duelling was done with pistols now, not swords, and it was banned in England, although still practised in the more backwards little countries of the Continent. I supposed one could possibly get one's nose shot off by a pistol. The Danish astronomer—I recalled his name now, Tycho Brahe—after his duel, had worn a nose made of sterling silver. I wondered why he had not chosen gold, which could hardly have been in worse taste, but I supposed people thought differently about such things before the reign of Queen Victoria. I supposed, now that I thought about it, there were likely a number of men in England whose faces had been similarly altered, if not in duels, then in wars: the Indian Mutiny, the Second Afghan War, that sort of thing. Surely they did not wear silver noses, or chins or ears as the case might be. What—

There came a timid knock at my chamber door, and my landlady's girl-of-all-work—a wretched wisp of a child who could not have been more than ten years old—asked, "Will you dine, Miss Everseau?"

"Yes, I will be down directly." While my current landlady's disposition was in wretched contrast to Mrs. Tupper's, the meals she served were far superior.

Meanwhile I sent the girl out for the evening papers, and when I returned to my room after an excellent dinner of roast lamb with mint sauce, I turned up the gas—what luxury to have such ease and effectiveness of lighting, even though the pipes hissed and muttered like a mumbling lunatic. Seated in the least uncomfortable chair, I read all the papers, checking first to see whether there had been any further developments in the Watson case—none were reported—and second to make sure my personal was included:

Hawthorn, convolvulus, asparagus and poppies:
what do you want? Reply this column. M.M.W.

It was.

Interesting, I thought, that the sender of the bizarre bouquets, letting alone the matter of his nose for the moment, should be a *man*. Flowers were generally considered to be in the female domain, although of course there were always a few eccentric amateur scientists, followers of Malthus and Darwin, trying to cross-pollinate orchids in hothouses. Also, upon further reflection, I supposed that any man who had ever courted and/or married necessarily learned something of the language of flowers. How fortunate for me that both my brothers were confirmed bachelors, thereby remaining ignorant. Undoubtedly Sherlock, keeping an eye on the personal advertisements for any demand regarding Watson, would notice "hawthorn, convolvulus, asparagus and poppies" and be intrigued, possibly even thinking, quite mistakenly, that it had something to do with Mother and me; I doubted he would guess nearer to the truth. In any event, I hoped for a response of some sort from the hawthorn man in the morning.

Meanwhile, I scanned the newspapers I had been too busy to read this morning and yesterday.

There were quite a lot to go through, and no particular reasons to do so except for the discipline of keeping up with the news. But after a while I found myself reading without comprehension, and occasionally one must make allowances. Yawning, I decided that after I finished looking at the "agony columns" of the *Pall Mall Gazette*, which I was reading at the moment, I would go ahead and throw the whole lot into the fire—

Just then I saw it.

66

422555 415144423451 334244542351545351
3532513451
35325143 23532551 55531534
3132345544411435432513
31533

Oh.

Oh, my goodness. Suddenly wide awake, with my heart thumping I reached for paper and pencil.

First I jotted down the alphabet, thus:

ABCDE FGHIJ KLMNO PQRST UVWXYZ

Then I started on the first word. Fourth line, second letter, Q. Second line, fifth letter, J.

QJ?

Realising my mistake, I started again. Fourth letter of the second line, I. Second letter of the fifth line, V. Fifth letter of the fifth line, Y.

IVY. Yes, it *was* for me.

The gas-light whispering in its pipes now sounded like a ghost in the room. A painful yet incorporeal corset tightened around my chest; I found it difficult to breathe properly as I continued deciphering. But it did not take long to complete the task.

IVY DESIRE MISTLETOE WHERE WHEN
LOVE YOUR CHRYSANTHEMUM

The best and the worst of all possible messages.

It seemed I could no longer put off thinking about my mother.

* * *

I slept very little that night. Indeed, had I not left all of my warm, concealing, dark clothing behind at Mrs. Tupper's, I would not have attempted to sleep at all; I would have roamed the city in search of those less fortunate than I, to give them food and shillings and think less of my own difficulties. Such nighttime questing was very much a custom of mine; a pox on Viola Everseau for keeping me from it. Instead, I needs must lie on a hard and narrow bed while my thoughts refused to be still, chasing around and around like noisy and undisciplined children.

Was there no order left in the universe? Mother had never initiated communication with me before. Always the other way around.

It was a trick. Just like the last time "Mama"—actually, my brother Sherlock—had arranged to rendezvous, except that now Sherlock had caught on to the code of flowers, saying "mistletoe" instead of "a meeting"—

But surely Sherlock would not be wasting any time on me right now, with Dr. Watson missing!

Perhaps it really was Mother.

If so, my mother must be in some sort of terrible trouble.

But wouldn't she name her own time and place if her need to see me were urgent?

If someone were setting a trap for me—letting me choose

where and when, wasn't that a way to lure me in?

Strictly speaking, Mother should not have said "mistletoe"; that meant a tryst between a gentleman and his paramour. Mother should have said "scarlet pimpernel."

Unless Mother simply thought "scarlet pimpernel" was too much to encrypt?

She could have put "pimpernel," a word no longer than "mistletoe."

Was that not what she would have done? Was the message fake, not from her at all, a trick?

But why? And by whom?

It was in the *Pall Mall Gazette* and no other newspapers. In Mother's favourite publication and no others.

It had to be from Mother. I wanted it to be from Mother.

I wanted to see Mother?

Yes.

No. No, I was angry with her, for good reason.

IVY DESIRE MISTLETOE WHERE WHEN LOVE YOUR CHRYSANTHEMUM

The message said "love."

Mother had never in her life said such a thing to me.

It was a trick.

It was what I had always wanted from her.

Either the message was a false one—but from whom?—or else my mother had found some affection for me in her heart after all.

If I did not respond, I would always wonder.

And if I did respond, I would be risking myself and my freedom for the sake of a single fickle word.

When one does not know what to do, prudence might decree that one should do nothing, but I cannot bear such inactivity. Hence my penchant to wander the night—and lacking that release, at dawn after a mostly sleepless night I got up and prepared to go out, even though I had no idea where or for what purpose. I donned my corset-armament-supplies-munitions, petticoats, then a frock sufficiently flounced, frilled, ruffled and beribboned to "promenade" city streets, and went on to beautify (in other words, totally disguise) my face. All the while my mind continued its interminable romping circles: Was the encrypted message truly from my mother? Should I reply to it? What would I say if, and when, I did?

For the time being, much as I disliked indecision, I would wait. That much I knew, for the only time I had called upon Mother for assistance she had made me wait—and wait—and wait some more; indeed she had not responded at all, and my resentment was such that I felt I *ought* not to see her until I had disciplined my feelings, lest I say something I might later regret. But at the same time, if she had now really and truly reached out to me, and I did not respond . . . What if she had been ill, and had only a brief time left to live? What if this was my last chance to make my peace with her?

Nonsense. If Mother were on her deathbed, she would hardly be asking me to name the time and place for a rendezvous!

But . . .

And but, and but, and so my thoughts ground round and round until, like a mill ox, they had worn their own tired path. I had all but forgotten about the missing Dr. Watson, the forlorn Mrs. Watson and the sender of bizarre bouquets, he of the most peculiar removeable proboscis.

Yet, as I glued my little birthmark onto my temple, up from some hidden kitchen in the cellar of my mind came elucidation on a silver platter, answering my barely asked question of the day before: What did men with faces disfigured by combat do to ameliorate or conceal the defect? Like a dumbwaiter opening to display a tray of éclairs, common sense served the answer: If one needed it, why not a false nose, or ear, whatever, realistically made of flesh-coloured rubber, and where would one obtain such a thing? Surely at one of the establishments dealing in face putty, skullcaps and other theatrical paraphernalia, or perhaps even at the shop where I had bought my birthmark and my wig.

Pertelote's.

Which used to be Chaunticleer's.

Salvation! Needing something to do right now, I would call there.

CHAPTER
THE
TENTH

IT IS MUCH TO THE CREDIT OF THE platter-faced proprietess that she did not gawk or exclaim as I entered Pertelote's. She only gazed, and murmured, "My goodness. Good 'eavens. And you carry it off splendidly. My congratulations, Miss, ah, Everseau."

So she recognised the wig and the birthmark, remembered my unprepossessing appearance at the time of our transactions, and even recalled the name she had imprinted upon my calling-cards.

"Thank you." I smiled. She knew as well as I did that the name I used was not my own, just as I was not what I appeared to be, but I heard nothing mocking, condescending or sly in her voice; hers was a warm sort of discretion, one might even say motherly—

As if Mother ever mothered me?

Do not think about Mother.

"'Ow may I 'elp you today?"

With some difficulty I disciplined my thoughts to attend to my business, which was to question Pertelote without appearing to do so. Therefore, I had to pretend to be in her shop for some other purpose. "The Spanish papers," I murmured. "I find them rather awkward. Have you anything . . . else . . ."

"Of course. This way."

She led me to a back alcove screened off from the rest of the shop, where she revealed to me a number of remarkable substances—liquid, paste and powdered—that could be discreetly used to enhance one's eyes. Eye-drops to increase brilliance. Eyelash augmentation to obviate the need for tasteless fakery. Eyelid and eyebrow glosses, "shadows," and pastel colouring.

"The secret," explained Pertelote, "is to use just a 'int. One's advantage is spoilt if one's 'and is detected."

Seated on a divine little lace-skirted dressing-chair at a well-lit mirror, dabbing miracle-working unguents onto my face as she directed me, I exclaimed, "Fascinating!"

"Quite so."

"Are these materials used in the theatre?"

"No, these are too subtle for the stage. These are rather recondite emollients, Miss Everseau. One might find them 'idden in the dressing-table drawers of countesses, duchesses, even queens."

Merest cant, of course, yet I found myself half believing her. Greatly impressed, I looked up at her plain large-featured face flanked by buns of grey hair. "I feel honoured. But how ever did you come to discover these?"

"Why, in the business way."

"But how came you into this sort of business?"

"One who is ugly beyond 'ope dealing in the secrets of beauty, you mean?" She uttered these shockingly frank words with a smile in which I saw not the slightest trace of bitterness, only amusement. "It is ironic, is it not."

Her extraordinary honesty both delighted and perplexed me. "That is not what I meant at all," I told her sincerely. "How does a woman come to undertake such a queer sort of shop as this?"

I noticed that—oddly, for such a forthright person—she hesitated slightly before telling me, "Oh, well, it was my 'usband's at first, you see."

"Ah! Chaunticleer was your husband?"

Chaunticleer could not by any stretch of fancy have been his real name, of course. I suppose that is why she smiled rather oddly.

I extrapolated further. "And was he an actor, or some such, that he entered into merchandising of this sort?"

"No, not at all." She seemed less and less inclined to answer my questions.

"But he has now, ah, passed away?" In the natural order of things she would have taken over the shop because she was widowed.

"No, 'e's retired."

Her tone attempted to put an end to my curiosity, but I refused to be quelled. "Truly? How delightful for him," I prattled. "How does he spend his time now?"

"Oh, in 'is precious 'ot'ouse." The answer shot out of

her in such a harsh tone, one would have thought he killed puppies for a pastime.

Hothouse?

I had come here intending somehow to find out whether she had any male customers who required false noses, but had found out instead that she had a husband who, perhaps, cultivated rather nasty flowers?

"You dislike the hothouse?" I inquired meekly.

"I dislike the 'usband," she answered, grimly yet with such disarming candour that we both laughed. Then she changed the subject. "Would you like to see the latest emollients to en'ance the lips, Miss Everseau?"

In order to placate her, I applied some rosy colour to my mouth, after which I selected amongst the "recondite emollients" she had showed me, making a purchase generous enough, I hoped, to make her think kindly of me. Once the items were done up in a brown paper parcel, I placed it in my string shopping bag, then hesitated in Pertelote's doorway at the moment of departure. It seemed to me that, having failed to work the conversation around to my objective, I must be direct, and that I must ask now or never.

"I wonder," I started in a by-the-bye sort of way, "do you ever have occasion, Mrs., ah . . ." My pause inquired her name.

"Kippersalt," she said, rather reluctantly.

"Ah. Mrs. Kippersalt, have you ever had occasion to provide false ears, perhaps, or fingers, for people who have lost their own?"

She started to nod and declare with some small pride, "Why, certainly—"

But I had not yet finished speaking. "Or a false nose, perhaps?"

Her nodding abruptly ceased, and her tone of voice turned sharp. "Why do you ask?"

"An acquaintance of mine has had a most interesting, if somewhat discomfiting, encounter with a man whose false nose came off," I said. "I just wondered—"

She burst out, "What's 'e done now?"

Interesting!

"Who?" I demanded.

"Never mind." Her usual smile had quite turned into a scowl, and suddenly conscious of her big-boned size and strength, I needed to discipline myself not to step away from her. All that was motherly about her had transformed to menace. "What yer prying for?" she demanded, her accent more Cockney by the moment, her fists on her ample hips as she glowered at me. "'Oo are you? Now ye know my name, what's yers?" Then, when I did not reply, "I don't want yer business! Get out and don't come 'ere again."

I did not linger to argue the point, but left with the most lively curiosity capering in my mind. I had, after all, come to Pertelote—Mrs. Kippersalt, I reminded myself, Kippersalt; I must remember that name—I had come only to see whether it was possible for a man with a missing nose to wear a rubber one, and, if so, did she know of any instances?

Well. It would certainly appear that she did, painfully so, and more so than she desired anyone to know, but what should I do about this?

Making my way down Holywell Street, I quite wanted to stop and sit somewhere to think, perhaps on paper—but I could not pause, indeed I hastened my pace, for despite my mental abstraction I had noticed quite a majority of masculine heads turning as I passed, numerous unsolicited greetings from the "gents" loitering around the print-shops, and a male pest following me—no, two of them! What in the name of Heaven—

Then I realised I was still wearing the lip colouring and various tints, "shadows," glosses, eyelash amplifier, et cetera that I had put on in Pertelote's hidden alcove.

Oh, dear. Men were such simpletons. The more artifice, the more they . . . such imbeciles, to be enchanted by a wig, some padding and a little paint. Had I rendered myself a bit *too* ravishing?

At last I reached the more spacious pavements of the Strand. Hurrying away from Holywell Street, searching for some place of refuge, I heard the familiar call of a boy with newspapers to sell: "Piper! Piper!" in a Cockney accent. Striding to where he stood, I flipped my penny into his waiting cap and took a newspaper, which I opened at once, standing where I was, simply to hide behind.

Having done so, by an effort of will I calmed my own breathing. As was my usual remedy in trying moments, I envisioned my mother's face and brought to mind her oft-repeated words to me: "Enola, you will do quite well on your own." But rather than settling me, the thought of Mother made my heart lurch, for that message—IVY DESIRE MISTLETOE WHERE WHEN LOVE YOUR CHRYSANTHEMUM—I had not yet replied—had it come from her or had it not?

Too many problems. What to do about Mother. What to do about the strange behaviour of Mrs. Kippersalt. What to do about the missing Dr. Watson. Scanning the "agony columns" of the newspaper I held, I looked for an answer to "Hawthorn, convolvulus, asparagus and poppies" and without much satisfaction I found it:

M.M.W.: Deadly nightshade. Thank Yew.

Not at all helpful. Only frightening.

The deadly nightshade, an attractive wildflower whose berries were poisonous, while not to be found in any of the usual lexicons of the meanings of bouquets, posed a clear enough threat by its name. The mocking insertion of yew, symbol of graveyards, made it even clearer: a death threat towards, presumably, poor Dr. Watson.

Good heavens, I had to do something, but what? Immobile behind my shielding newspaper, I stood trying to think, but found it almost impossible to formulate any rational plan when, out of the corners of my eyes, I glimpsed masculine forms lingering nearby, ogling me, and knew they intended to follow me—although I still found it difficult to believe what fools the generality of men were! But experience forced me to conclude that the sight of a pretty woman turned

78

most of them into jackasses. Why, look at how the male clerks in the newspaper offices had changed their manner towards me when I—

A most illuminating thought opened my eyes wide.

Male clerks.

Newspaper offices.

Hmm. Chancy—for I lacked experience in the feminine art of flirtation—but certainly worth a try. I had nothing to lose by the attempt.

Folding my newspaper and thrusting it into my string bag along with my parcel, I strode to the nearest cab-stand, ignoring the pests trailing me. Selecting a four-wheeler in which to conceal myself, I told the driver, "Fleet Street."

CHAPTER
THE
ELEVENTH

EN ROUTE, I SET MY PLANS IN ORDER IN my mind. The object of my sortie was twofold: to learn a description, if not the actual identity, of the person who had placed "Deadly nightshade, thank Yew"—but also to try to find out whether it had indeed been my Mother who had sent the message "desire mistletoe" to me.

I decided I must address the matter of the bizarre bouquets first, for Dr. Watson's life might well be at stake. Secondarily, I admitted to another, selfish reason: Assuming that "Deadly nightshade, thank Yew" had been placed in all the newspapers, I would have several opportunities to try out my plan—but 422555 415144423451 et cetera (IVY DESIRE MISTLETOE) having appeared only in the *Pall Mall Gazette*, I must know what I was doing by the time I got there.

In the privacy of the cab I extracted scissors from my bust in order to clip today's message from my newspaper before discarding the latter. Then, at the busiest corner of

Fleet Street (for I did not wish to be noticed) I rapped on the roof of the cab to bid the driver to stop. After paying my fare, I walked a few steps to the nearest newspaper office (it happened to be the *Daily Telegraph*) and approached the desk, where a young man of the "gent" persuasion was diddling with pen and blotter.

"Excuse me," I lisped in the wispiest voice I could manage.

He glanced up quite indifferently, but upon taking in my pulchritude of person, he straightened to attention like a bird dog on point.

Cooing, "Would you happen to remember who placed this personal advertisement?" I showed him my clipping.

"I, um . . ." With difficulty he managed to read it and ogle me at the same time. "Deadly nightshade, thank Yew. Ah, yes, that is an odd one. I seem to recall—"

"We do not give out such information," interrupted quite a starchy female voice; I glanced up to find an older woman in (also starchy) bombazine, obviously a supervisor, standing by. She glowered down upon the young fellow at the desk, but directed her remarks towards me, scolding as if I were a schoolchild, "If you were to place a personal advertisement, you would not desire to have your identity disclosed, now, would you?"

Taking my clipping back from the hapless clerk, I turned and exited with such dignity as I could muster. So much for the *Daily Telegraph*.

I proceeded towards the next newspaper office.

Quite a long day ensued. I will spare the gentle reader a full account of my rebuffs and near triumphs other than to say that, in general, males welcomed me and females did not; very much the opposite. I did manage to obtain a little information when males, but not females, were present. In two instances, young men—I cannot say gentlemen, as they implied that I owed them a certain familiarity in return—indeed I felt much mortified as I wheedled information out of them, but putting aside my maidenly revulsion, I found reason for satisfaction: Their accounts tallied. The "deadly nightshade" advertisement, they both said, had been placed by a most peculiar man with a grey goatee, wearing a top-hat although he seemed not to be upper class, evidently trying to make himself appear taller, for he was slight of height, stark-boned and altogether rather repulsive. Pressed as to what exactly, other than his lack of stature, caused this impression, they replied that he looked odd—"cadaverous," said one. "Like a leper," said the other. Asked how so, he seemed rather at a loss, but explained that there was something odd about the man's face.

"Kind of like a dummy made of wax, if you've ever seen any such."

It seemed to me that they might very well be depicting "just a long-faced tove in chin-whiskers 'n a top-hat, excepting that 'e took 'is nose off," as a much-perturbed street urchin had once told me—a man with a false nose glued on, the juncture disguised with face putty. Such artifice might give his features a subtly disturbing tone, texture and rigidity.

Given what I had learned, I felt it safe to surmise that

the sender of bizarre bouquets had indeed answered my advertisement, and while gratified to verify his existence, I worried: How to find this most interesting individual?

I had no idea.

Except that Pertelote—Mrs. Kippersalt—might know something of him, having reacted so oddly to my questions. "What's 'e done now?" And having then angrily banned me from her shop.

Hmm.

I quite wanted to know where the Kippersalts lived and see whether Mr. Kippersalt cultivated hawthorn in his hothouse—indeed, I much desired a look at Mr. Kippersalt himself, to see whether his face seemed long, leprous, cadaverous, waxen, et cetera.

Might I find him by following Mrs. Kippersalt home after her work?

Not tenable, I decided after brief consideration. At this time of year, darkness had not yet fallen when the shops were closed, and if Mrs. Kippersalt were to catch sight of me, no matter how I dressed she would recognise me, having seen me in so many guises already. Also, I had no desire to repeat the adventure of "shadowing" someone. The last time, walking in the street to avoid the lamplight of the pavements, I had nearly been flattened by a Clydesdale pulling a lumber-wagon.

No. I needed to find Mr. Kippersalt by other means.

Kippersalt: Not a common surname, and locating his place of residence should have been simple enough were London run like a sensible city, but it was not. Indeed, the world's largest metropolis was also the world's worst governed. London was organised—or, more properly, disorganised—into more than two hundred boroughs, each with its own records-keeper, tax-collector, constables, et cetera.

However, hypothesising that the Kippersalts lived not far from their shop—as was most often the case with older people engaged in commerce that had been established before the Underground had begun to whisk workers from the outskirts of London into the City—*if* the Kippersalts lived on Holywell Street or not far away, I might visit only two or three borough offices before I obtained some information.

As these thoughts occupied my mind, my footsteps took me back down Fleet Street towards the one newspaper office I had not yet visited: that of the *Pall Mall Gazette*.

As I entered, my heart sank, for I saw that a stiff and spinsterly woman sat behind the desk.

Just the same, I had to try. On the window ledge lay copies of the paper for the last several days. With my foolish heart pounding beneath the dagger concealed in my dress-front, I located the one I needed, opening it to find amongst the personal advertisements.

422555 415144423451 334244542351
5453513532513451 35325143 2353 2551
55531534 313234 55441143543251331533
(IVY DESIRE MISTLETOE WHERE WHEN
LOVE YOUR CHRYSANTHEMUM).

Pointing it out to the dry stick of a woman behind the desk, I asked—indeed, I begged—"Could you tell me who placed this?"

"Indeed I could not," she rapped out in answer.

Could not, or would not? She seemed quite the virgin queen of her small realm, one who would know everything.

I tried again. "Might you tell me, at least, whether it was a man or a woman?" If it was a woman, it had to be Mother.

And as I thought this, my heart froze, for if it were so, I still did not know how to respond.

But the old maid behind the desk snapped, "I can tell you nothing."

I offered a bribe; she reacted angrily. Still, I pleaded with her for several minutes longer. Only when she threatened to summon a constable did I leave the office.

Very well, I had done my best.

Although some invisible cook seemed to be mixing a very strange pudding of emotion in my chest—was I distraught that I had found out nothing, or relieved?—yet in my thoughts I pushed Mother away for the time being.

There was a much more pressing matter to be attended to.

A deadly one, thank Yew.

Some hours later, I entered the humble abode of the much-bewildered Mrs. Tupper, who blinked several times when she saw me come in.

"Miss Meshle," she asked uncertainly, "would you like some supper?"

"No, thank you, Mrs. Tupper." I was in a great hurry to change into dark, inconspicuous clothing. "I have no time." This fact did not improve my humour, for I felt as hollow as a drum, having missed luncheon as well.

"Eh?" The deaf old soul placed her hearing-trumpet to her ear.

"No! Thank you! Mrs. Tupper!" For once shouting was not a nuisance, but a relief to my feelings. My feet hurt abominably from slogging up and down Fleet Street *plus* visiting eight—no, ten—I had lost count—an inordinate number of borough offices without locating a single Kippersalt except one Augustus Kippersalt, who had been put away in Colney Hatch Lunatic Asylum; he could not possibly be my man. Altogether, it had been a most trying day.

My only hope, then, was—after all—to get back to Pertelote's by the time that much-ruffled oversized hen of a woman put her shutters up, to see where she went.

Limping upstairs to my room, I relieved my suffering feet of my unfortunately fashionable boots. I snatched off my wig and sloughed off my dress—peach-coloured taffeta interlaced with white "baby" ribbons, most unsuitable for concealment—then yanked a dark, commonplace woollen blouse and skirt out of my wardrobe to put on. I slipped my blistered feet into thick socks, then my blessedly comfortable old black boots. Having no time to wash the "recondite emollients" off my face, I smeared ashes from the hearth upon myself. Transformed thus to quite a commonplace Sally-down-the-alley, I sheathed my longest dagger in the front of my corset, grabbed for a rusty black shawl to throw over my head, and ran back downstairs, feeling rather than facing Mrs. Tupper's puzzled gaze as I bolted out the door.

CHAPTER
THE
TWELFTH

"CAB!" I YELLED IMPERIOUSLY AT the first opportunity. The driver, although no society prize himself, turned incredulously upon being hailed by an apparent woman of the slums. "Yer addressin' me?"

I tossed him a golden coin, which instantly silenced his doubts and objections. "The Strand at St. Mary's," I told him as I climbed in, that corner being close enough to Holywell Street; he must not know where I was actually going. "And another sovereign if you get me there in ten minutes."

"Yes, *ma'am*!" Plentiful cash-at-hand worked better than ravishing beauty to transform one's status, under certain circumstances. "I'm your man. Me and old Conductor 'ere, we'll see you there." As he whipped his wretched ewe-necked nag into a rapid trot, I tried not to think of anything I had ever read in *Black Beauty*, sitting back, bracing myself against the swaying of the conveyance and disciplining myself to consider instead what lay ahead.

I disliked rushing in such a headlong fashion into I knew not quite what, but I felt I must seize the moment, for in Pertelote's—that is to say, in Mrs. Kippersalt's anger I sensed an opportunity that might not occur again.

I was going to have to try to "shadow" her home after all, because she would take her anger along with her when she went there. She would direct her ire at her husband—"What 'ave ye done now?" And I quite wanted somehow, I did not yet know how, to hear the answer.

Moreover, I needed to look at Mr. Kippersalt. I had spent a great deal of imagination upon Mr. Kippersalt, and seeing him would either support or disprove my hypotheses, which were:

Suppose that a man, in war or in some unfortunate accident, had his face maimed, including but not limited to his nose.

Suppose that, in attempting to find ways to conceal the defects in his appearance, he became an expert in face putty, rubber features and the like; might he not open a shop specialising in these things, if only to obtain them readily for himself?

Being quite an unprepossessing man, might he not, for the sake of housekeeping and so on, marry an exceedingly plain woman who had no other prospects?

Perhaps an ambitious Cockney woman?

Having wed him not for love but for self-advancement, might this unusual woman improve herself to the extent that eventually she took over the running of the shop?

Might he not resent being pushed aside? Resent it to such an extent that he—

That he did what? Avenged himself upon Dr. Watson?

Whatever grudge could he possibly hold against Dr. Watson?

But wait a moment. Perhaps he blamed Watson for the loss of his nose? Suppose it had happened during the second Afghan War, in which Watson had served as an army surgeon? Perhaps Watson had amputated his wounded proboscis?

Brilliant, I congratulated myself mentally, pleased and excited to have hit upon such a plausible connection.

The speeding, swaying, veering cab in which I sat pulled to a jouncing halt at my destination.

I burst out before the wheels had quite come to rest, leaping into a full-tilt run as I threw the cabbie a sovereign even though I had no clock to tell me—had he got me here quickly enough?

He had.

Panting, I poked my head around the corner of Holywell Street just in time to see Mrs. Kippersalt closing the last shutters to secure her shop for the night. Then she went back inside to fasten them.

The last rays of daylight—blessed, sunny light most uncommon in London—lingered on the peaked roofs of the crowded old buildings as I waited, watching the door, expecting it to open and her to emerge with coat and hat, gloves and umbrella, to lock up and start homeward.

Daylight turned to dusk, and I still waited.

Mrs. Kippersalt had not come back out.

What ever in the world had become of her? Perhaps—oh, good heavens, no—she had gone out a back way?

Quite unlikely, for Holywell Street meandered along the edge of London's most dense, clotted "rookery," tottering houses shouldering one another, each containing a swarming "nest" of poverty-stricken inhabitants. Spaces—no, indeed, tunnels, for the upper storeys closed together overhead—passageways no wider than gutters separated these buildings from one another, unlit, and no cleaner than gutters either, with rats abounding, as well as lower forms of human life. Inconceivable that Mrs. Kippersalt would venture alone into such a sewer-above-the-ground unless she looked forward to the attentions of Jack the Ripper or like-minded others.

Inconceivable that she could have slipped away without my seeing her.

Yet with each passing moment it seemed more and more evident that she had done so, and that I was a fool. And I called myself a perditorian? No, I was a mere girl, more fit to cut out paper dolls, I despaired as dusk deepened into dark. Lamplight glowed from rooms up above, but it did not comfort me, serving only to cast me into deeper shadow, for these ancient buildings loomed like a sea-carved cliff, their upper storeys jutting out over the pavement, gables protruding, each floor with eaves and bay windows overhanging the one below, so that they seemed built upside down, larger at the top than at the bottom, and likely to crash down upon one at any moment.

Like my little struggling self-made world. I tried to do things and find missing people, but to what effect? Here

I stood in the dark, alone, cast aside by my own mother, feeling wretched enough to mew like a lost kitten—

A glow of lamplight sprang to life in the first storey over Pertelote's. Light sprang to life in my mind, also, as it were. My melodramatic musings abruptly ceased. The next moment, abandoning misery along with concealment, I ran across the street—unpeopled now that the shop-windows stood dark—and up the pavement to Pertelote's.

If that were she up there in the room over the pavement, the room under which swung the sign carved in the shape of a cockerel—if, as might very well be the case, why had I not thought of it before!—she lived over her shop—

I had to see.

Quickly. Already they were quarrelling—yes, it was Pertelote in the upstairs room; I recognised her contralto voice—she and someone else were arguing vehemently. Through a partially open window I could hear their angry tones from where I stood, although I could not catch the words.

I had to get closer.

But how?

I saw within a moment how to start, at least. Taking three quick strides to the shadowy, stinking gutter-gap between Pertelote's and the next shop, I yanked my skirt above my knees, and by pressing parts of my personage against the opposing walls—truly, I cannot with decency detail how I ascended the narrow space, except to say that up I went rather like a sweep inside a chimney.

After the first six feet or so I felt small fear that anyone who might happen to pass by would spy me, for who would look upwards to notice a girl in such an unlikely position?

As my head neared the level of the gas-lit window, I could hear Pertelote more clearly. "You think I'm a fool? Ye're up to some mischief, gadding about when my back's turned. I want to know what."

"I told you. Taking care of my own business."

Wait a moment. The second voice, husky and low, sounded almost exactly like the first. Two women. Who was the other?

Where was Pertelote's husband?

Pertelote scolded, "You got no business but to stay home and don't plant no more people."

"I didn't plant nobody. Just filled out some papers to put 'im where 'e put me. The place'll do for 'im."

I heard a gasp of shock, then Pertelote all but screamed, "You're mad as an 'atter! Me 'usband was right to 'ave you put away!"

"But you made 'im get me out again, didn't you?"

"Shut your wicked mouth. You—"

"You made 'im get me out again," insisted the second woman, "because ye can take care of me at 'ome 'ere. Ye'll always take care of me, won't ye, Sissy?"

Something about the voice—not merely its peevish tone, but something as implacable as time—made the hairs prickle on the nape of my neck.

I had reached the limits of my "chimney," the point at which the buildings' walls joined together, and the window from which the voices issued remained above me and off to one side. I could hear but I could not see.

I had to see. See who was speaking. See who was so obstinately repeating, "Ye'll always take care of me, I said; answer me. I know ye'll always take care of me."

Like a horizontal wall between me and that window jutted the eaves that sheltered the pavement below.

Quite hard, that pavement. Most unrelenting to fall upon. Nevertheless . . .

I took a deep breath. Then I leaned out over the dark abyss, grasped the rounded wooden edge of the eaves with both hands, and kicked away from the safety of my "chimney," trying to swing myself upwards and onto the confounded obstacle.

I succeeded in throwing one knee over. However, at the same time, one hand lost its grip.

A knee, I quickly discovered, does not function as well as a hand under such circumstances. It slipped off. I had to exercise every iota of self-will not to scream.

"Ye'll always take care of me, won't ye, sister mine?" insisted the relentless contralto voice. "Say it. Ye'll always take care of me."

Would that someone might take care of *me*! Catching hold of the too-smooth edge of the eaves again with my other hand, I hoisted myself with strength spurred by panic, and managed to get the upper portion of my personage over the top, then my lower limbs, then roll away from the edge. Panting, I found myself lying on a slantwise sort of ledge.

"Ye'll always take care of me," that fanatical voice went on, singsong, as I sprawled, gasping for breath, scared half out of my wits, and that voice added frisson to my fear. Each word chilled me. Not only the tone, but the substance: *take care of me, take care of me*—it was, in the heart of my heart, what I had always wanted—of my family . . .

"Ye'll always take care of me, won't ye, sister mine? Say it! Ye'll always take care of me."

"Of course I will always take care of you," Pertelote snapped finally. "I always 'ave done, 'aven't I?"

Triumphantly the other responded, "Not when ye let the rats eat me face."

CHAPTER
THE
THIRTEENTH

RATS. EAT. FACE.

If she'd said it a moment earlier, before I'd gained the ledge, I believe I would have lost my grip and fallen to nearly certain death on the pavement below. As it was, I flattened myself like a squirrel as the falcon flies overhead, trembling, my fingers clutching at the shingles and my thoughts clawing at an even more slippery slope.

"That was forty years ago." Pertelote's weary voice.

"Forty-two," complained the other, and in her ever-so-accurate spleen I recognised, with revulsion, something of myself.

The way I was holding a grudge.

Mother. Mother.

I'd long ago forgiven her for going away, free spirit that she was. She had provided for me. We communicated by code in the personal columns of the newspapers. But two months ago, on one of the coldest days in January, feeling a bit desperate, I had asked her to come into London to meet me. How it hurt, still, that she had not even replied.

"I was only five years old," responded Pertelote wearily. "I fell asleep."

"And I was only a baby," retorted the other, "'elpless in the cradle, and ye let the rats crawl on me and nibble me nose off—"

"Stop it, Flora."

But Flora's drone did not hesitate for so much as a syllable. "—and me lips, and the better part of me cheeks—"

"Stop it!"

"—and ye were supposed to be watching me—"

Yes, she too wanted to be taken care of, living with her sister, how comforting it should have been, sisters together. I'd never had a sister. I—

Was I about to tell myself I had always wanted a sister?

Nonsense, Enola. You never till this minute even thought of it.

As for being taken care of: I had two brothers quite eager to take care of me by having me schooled in the social graces and rendered fit for matrimony. And I had a mother who had taken care of me by giving me freedom and the means to employ myself as I saw fit.

Stop feeling sorry for yourself, Enola Holmes. You'll do quite well on your own.

That inner voice, kind yet firm—it was my own, yet it was as if Mother were still with me. In me. And in that moment quite willingly I forgave her for being the way she was.

A weight flew away from my heart.

Meanwhile, Flora was still complaining, "Ye're my big sister, supposed to take care of me, and ye're saying I didn't cry loud enough to awaken ye?"

Her lament sounded merely wearisome to me now.

But even though Pertelote must have heard it many, many times before, it affected her. "For the love of God, Flora, stop!" she flared with pain in her voice. "You're cruel!"

"It's me 'oo's missing a nose, Sissy, not you."

Nose.

Oh, my goodness.

No longer flattened or trembling, I lifted my head, for I quite wanted a look at Flora. With my mind once again focused on the present circumstances, I realised that my brilliant theory of a soldier who'd had his nose amputated by Dr. Watson needed to be discarded, even though it was a man who had sent the bizarre bouquets—

Or was it? I had to see whether Flora might pass as a man.

Easing myself to my hands and knees, I crept (mentally excoriating my skirt; most difficult to crawl in) along the ledge as silently as I could, towards the window.

Pertelote said, "Ever since Ma died I've done my best for you."

Very likely true. From my first acquaintance with Pertelote, she had seemed motherly to me. Evidently she had taken the responsibilities of a mother at an early age.

At the corner of the window I inched my head upwards until I could see—not much, at first. Lace curtains. But by leaning forward I could peer through them, albeit dimly. I could make out a drab and shabby chamber within, a sitting-room, although neither sister occupied a chair; their passions had levitated them to their feet. Pertelote stood with her back to me, fists on her ample hips, partly hiding Flora from my view. I could tell of Flora only that she was sturdy, like her sister, and plainly dressed in blouse and skirt, like Pertelote again. Although I imagined Flora's face would similarly be large and plain, I could not see her features.

And it was Pertelote doing the ranting now. "All my life since, always trying to make it up to you," she cried, "always! Got my 'usband into the business looking for ways to make you presentable—"

"Ye were just trying to marry me off and get rid of me."

"I were trying to make ye 'appy, and a decent woman, but you 'ad to go and put on a beard an' trousers—"

Oh. Oh, my, she *was* the sender of the bizarre bouquets; she had to be. In a fever to see her face, I pressed close to the outside of the window glass.

"—gadding about doing the devil knows what," Pertelote raged.

"I had to act the part of yer 'usband, now, didn't I?"

"No, you didn't! You don't want to let 'im rest in peace, you're just wicked and full of 'ate—"

"*You* try being 'ideous." Heavens, the afflicted woman pitied herself. She needed some starch. "At least a *man* is allowed—"

"—going against nature, 'ow many times 'ave I told you to stay 'ome when I'm working? But now I 'ear you're up to your tricks still! I've 'alf a mind to send you back to Colney 'Atch myself!"

99

The other one screeched in rage, lunging at her sister, and—I could see her face now, but I wished I couldn't, for she snatched off her nose with one hand and thrust it at Pertelote, shaking it like a weapon as she screamed, "You try it and see what 'appens! You just try it!" With her other hand she ripped rags of concealing putty off her mouth and cheeks. Her face, or what was left of it, writhed like a mass of slugs. "You'll be sorry! You and any doctor 'oo signs an order for you!"

I barely comprehended what Flora was saying, so terribly did the sight of her unnerve me—to see, instead of a face, crawling flesh; instead of mouth and nose, merest cavities. And her eyes—there was nothing wrong with her eyes except that, I think, they had forgotten how to weep, and murder glittered in their glare. The sight of those sere eyes affected me as much as the sight of her maimed face; I think I must have moved or made a sound, for her crazed gaze swung and caught upon me.

Caught me at the window like a great stupid fish drawn by a lighted torch to the surface of a nighttime lake.

She screamed as if she were seeing a—a mass of writhing slugs, I suppose—and pointed at me.

Just as Pertelote swung around to look at me also, I ducked.

One of the sisters, I know not which, shouted something quite shockingly unrepeatable.

I fled. But on that narrow ledge I could not turn quickly, if at all, so I could not go back the way I had come. Instead I scooted forward, around the corner of the building,

100

towards I knew not what. Along the eaves like an oversized caterpillar I wobbled, trying to crawl but hampered, indeed nearly thrown over the edge by my accursed skirt. I firmly believe that the whole reason women *must* wear long skirts is so that they are unable to *do* anything worthwhile.

Behind me I heard the window wham open and Pertelote, I think, bayed in a voice worthy of a whole pack of hounds, "Police! Help! Burglar! Police!"

A constable's whistle shrilled from the street, summoning others of his ilk. Answering whistles sounded to the north, west and east. From inside the building I heard the pounding of feet on stairs, going down.

They expected me to run away the same way. Go down.

Therefore I would not. I would go up.

Easier said than done, with a skirt wrapped around my ankles, and no light by which to see. But at the next corner my fumbling progress encountered a drain-pipe, and I seized upon it with both hands, hauling myself skywards like a sailor swarming up a mast. Meanwhile, below me, neighbours took to the street, police arrived and the hullabaloo—shouts, screams, whistles, clatter of hooves and thud of running feet—frightened out of me such strength as I had not thought I possessed. I reached the top of the drain-pipe only to be blocked by yet another beetling overhang of the cliff-like building, but somehow in my frenzy, like a cat when the mastiff threatens, I scrambled up and over it without hesitating.

And encountered yet another wall. Would I never reach the refuge of the rooftops? For a moment, out of utter frustration, I beat against the ancient plaster with my hands, but that was a useless waste of time and effort. I turned away from the street and ran along the narrow eaves in the dark. Ran. I did not creep or crawl as I had so cautiously done a few moments before, nor, preferring to remain on my feet, did I edge or inch in any sane fashion such as would have been appropriate to the circumstances. I ran, unable to see upon what my feet were landing. Perhaps lunacy is contagious.

With considerable force I banged into rough wood.

I am afraid I muttered something quite naughty as the barrier, whatever it was, inflicted its presence upon my nose, which as usual had arrived where I was going ahead of the rest of me. My hands quite wanted to comfort the nose, but I made them instead explore the structure that thwarted me.

It might have been the side of a bay window.

Ours not to wonder why; ours but to do or die; into the valley of death charged—no, onto the rooftop of desperation climbed the idiot who ought to be thankful for possession of a nose however protuberant; onwards and upwards, excelsior! Scrabbling to ascend the whatever-it-was, I clambered to its narrow top and, standing there, took a deep and thankful breath, for I could see now, albeit dimly.

I could see intimations of sky freckled with stars.

And against it, interruptions in the form of peaks and chimney-pots.

At last!

One more mad scramble over one final confoundment of jutting eaves, and I had achieved the roof.

Panting, I let myself lapse onto the steeply angled shingles, lying flat.

Safe.

No one could possibly find me now. I would simply rest here until daybreak.

But even as I thought it, in the street far below a sergeantly voice bawled, "Wheel it around this side! Over 'ere! 'Ow do you work the fool thing?"

The next moment the most extraordinary blinding-bright white sword of light stabbed the darkness, slashing it wide open and routing night into fleeing shadows. I had read in the newspapers, of course, about Scotland Yard's new electric search-light, but reading is one thing and being struck by such lightning is another. I am afraid I screamed aloud. However, so did everyone else in the world, or at least everyone in the crowded street below—so I think no one heard me.

"Tilt it up towards the roof!"

"'E's crazy," some other man announced. "No one could 'ave climbed up there, much less a woman—"

But I did not stay to listen. Much shaken and feeling a trifle weak, I did not attempt to stand and run on the steep rooftop, instead worming my way up the shingles—a most fortunate if unreasoning reaction; I realised afterwards that they might have "spotted" me otherwise.

However thin I might be, I do not make a very good snake. Still, somehow I reached the peak of Pertelote's building and, hugging the housetop, slipped over it to the other side.

That fearsome sword of illumination passed where I had just been. Safe on the shadowed side of the roof now, I watched it slice the night.

No, not safe. Next they would wheel it around to this side.

The thought, quite as electric as the light, galvanised me; I must reach another building, and another after that, and so make my escape. Springing to my feet, I ran across the steep slope of the roof towards the rear, away from that dreadful search-light, so bright that even in the shadows I could somewhat see where I was going. There! This rooftop joined directly into another not so steep. Gladly I sprang upon it—

Crash, and I plummeted straight down as if I had stepped off a ledge into air.

CHAPTER
THE
FOURTEENTH

AMIDST A CASCADING CHORUS, unmistakably the sound of broken glass, I plunged. Without my permission my mouth opened to scream.

But before it could do so, my benighted fall ended, *whump*, in something that cushioned the impact quite effectively.

I landed on my feet, buckled to my knees, and stayed that way amidst—what?

Some poufy, airy, springy substance like a giant bustle-pad. Much harder to identify in total darkness than the glass showering around me with a muffled splashing sound.

I tasted some salty, rather sticky liquid in my open mouth. Ordering the latter to close, I applied my sleeve to the former; yes, it hurt a bit. Blood. A shard of glass had cut my face, evidently. I felt some similar cuts, stinging so that I knew they could not be dangerously deep, on my hands.

All in all, however, it seemed to me that I had come off rather well. My bleeding, although upsetting, was not significant. The search-light would not find me here. I had fallen, I realised with a pang of annoyance at myself for being so stupid, through the roof of Mr. Kippersalt's hothouse, which of course occupied the very top of the building.

Mr. Kippersalt's? But Flora spoke as if he were dead. Moreover, if she were the origin of the bizarre bouquets, one must deduce that this was *her* hothouse.

As these thoughts arranged themselves in my rather disordered mind, I stayed perfectly still, listening in case someone came running to see what the noise had been about. But I heard nothing except my own pounding heart and panting breath, both gradually calming as nothing alarming happened. After a bit, it seemed safe to think that my pursuers remained on the street, and had not heard breaking glass amidst the hubbub there.

Well. Being in a hothouse, I must have landed in a large plant, blessedly pliant—I could feel its stems bending under me—not a giant bustle-pad at all, although its spidery fronds all around me itched and tickled like so much horsehair.

Still listening for any danger approaching, I explored with my hands, finding nothing within arm's length anywhere around me except more poufy vegetation. Quite large, this plant, whatever it was, brushing my face whilst my knees rested upon the potting soil in which it grew.

Just as I realised I was now safe—comparatively speaking— my entire personage was seized by a fit of trembling that would not listen to reason, and I felt as if I could no longer remain upright. Allowing myself to slump to the ground,

I burrowed between stems that gently yielded to me while the feathery fronds closed overhead. Stretched out at full length, still I found no end to—what? Most perplexing, as if I had somehow fallen into a jungle.

Wherever I was, I quite needed to rest for a few minutes. Just a little while, until my fit of "the shakes" ceased, and then I would get away. Quaking, I lay with both hands on my chest—that is to say, on the hilt of my dagger—and closed my eyes.

"Bloody blue blazes!" someone screamed. Or something of the sort. I think that's what she said. One hesitates to admit that one could have fallen asleep; indeed, one almost wishes to say that one fainted, except that it could not possibly be true, as I never faint . . . in any event, I opened my eyes to find myself looking up at the wan light of dawn filtering greenly between a great many delicate fronds of—simple enough to tell what it was now that I could see it. I lay engulfed in bushes and bushes of asparagus.

"My *babies*!" some woman, presumably Flora, was shrieking. "My 'awthorn, my trumpet flowers, my 'arebells, glass everywhere and the cold wind gusting in!"

While ashamed to confess that I'd let myself be taken so off guard, I can at least say that I retained the sense to lie utterly still—except that my fingers tightened around my dagger hilt—and make no sound.

Meanwhile, footfalls pounded up a nearby staircase.

"The villain!" continued the shrieker. "She broke in *'ere*! My 'ot'ouse!"

"Flora, calm yourself." Pertelote's weary voice. "She's long gone."

Would that it were so.

"Who the 'ell is she?" Indeed such was the profanity with which Flora spoke. "What's she want with us?"

"I don't know." Pertelote sounded unsurprised at her sister's language, but quite grim as she added, "I wish I did know."

"I'll kill 'er! I'll find 'er and I'll kill 'er like I killed—"

"*Flora!*" The force of Pertelote's rebuke commanded a halt to such talk, and received it. "You are to kill *no one*. No one ever again. *Do you 'ear me?*"

Flora muttered some sulky reply, inaudible to me.

In heightened tones Pertelote demanded, "What was that? *What 'ave you done with Dr. Watson?*"

"Nuthin. 'Oo said I done anything?" Flora whined like a child who, denied a tantrum, resorts to tears. "Why you got to bark at me after what 'appened to my *'ot'ouse?*"

"Oh, for the love of mercy, that's easily remedied. Send for the glazier." Pertelote sounded exhausted and disgusted. "You'd better not 'ave anything to do with whatever 'appened to Dr. Watson. My breakfast is getting cold." The sound of heavy steps signalled her departure.

"Thinks she can turn 'er back on me," Flora said, sniffling, to her "babies," I suppose. "Breakfast, indeed. I'm not finished, I'm not." I heard her thump off after her sister, slamming the hothouse door behind her.

Leaving me hidden, yet trapped, in a great deal of asparagus, where once again I started trembling.

Enola, this will not do.

But—the brusque, almost offhand mention of killing, and of Dr. Watson—

Think about that later. Think now how to get out of here.

My shaking increased.

In order to calm myself, as I had done so often before I closed my eyes and envisioned my mother's face. Of course she was saying, "Enola, you will do quite well on your own." Blessedly, the thought of her no longer hurt my heart, only warmed it, and stopped my quaking at once, so that I was able again to think clearly, to plan what to do.

It was, after all, not so difficult. I merely sat up amidst the asparagus, removed my boots so that I should be able to walk silently in my stocking feet, then got out of the asparagus, which grew in quite a massive, eight-foot-long galvanised steel container supported above the floor by several sawhorses. This I saw after I had climbed down and stepped softly away. I saw also the hole I had made in the roof by my involuntary entry, and broken glass scattered on asparagus, red hawthorn, white poppies . . . but I could not spare much attention for the hothouse, because I found myself swaying on my feet—understandably so, I realised. I had not eaten in twenty-four hours. And, reaching into my skirt pockets for the strengthening sweets I customarily carried with me, I found none; I had been in too much of a hurry, and had forgotten them.

Confound everything. I needed to make a quick escape, before I keeled over.

Carrying my boots, I padded—as silently as I could, in

109

my wobbly condition—to the hothouse door, where I halted and listened.

As I had hoped, I could hear the two sisters' quarrelling voices below. As long as they continued to berate one another, I would know where both were. And any servants would no doubt be busy eavesdropping.

Although, on second thought, I doubted there were any servants. If Flora was all that she seemed to be, Pertelote could not risk having "'elp," lest someone find out too much.

Very quietly I opened the hothouse door, then slipped out and down the stairs.

In a front room somewhere Flora was clamouring, "Ye'll always take care of me, won't ye, Sissy? Answer me. Ye'll always take care of me."

Except the time the rats ate her face.

Feeling very cold as well as very shaky, I crept down more back stairs, through an empty kitchen, out a back door, and then I ran, tottering, not caring that the stones bruised my feet or that I was fleeing into the worst thug-rookery in London City.

CHAPTER
THE
FIFTEENTH

QUAINTLY ENOUGH, MY DIRTY and dishevelled appearance served to protect me in these low, swarming streets. Last night's drunkards groaned in the gutters. A girl in a grimy pinafore and not much else huddled in a doorway, her bare feet blue with cold. Boys in shabby shirts and trousers enormously too big for them, rolled up like life-belts around their twiggy limbs, ran after a well-upholstered woman, begging for pennies. Wives emptied slops, flannel-vested workmen trudged about their business; a man with a push-cart shouted, "'Ot buns, sausage, suet pudding! 'Ot fat pudding fer yer breakfast!" No one paid me any attention as I sat on the kerb of a pavement to put my boots back on, or as I purchased from the street vendor an unspeakably vile sausage at which I gnawed while I limped along. Had the lovely Miss Everseau minced into these brawling thief-ridden streets, she would at once have been set upon, robbed, stripped of her fine clothing and let go naked if at all. But a frowsy-haired, wild-eyed, cut and bruised young woman who looked as if she had been in a fight was not noticed whatsoever.

When I arrived back at my lodging, however—the one on Dr. Watson's street, being a great deal closer at hand—matters were different. Luckily, the sharp-eyed landlady happened to be out, but I found it necessary to bribe the gawking young girl-of-all-work into silence with a shilling, and a promise of more should she tell her mistress only that I was unwell and required my meals to be brought up to my room. And yet another shilling to provide me with a bath, but say nothing of it.

Thus it was that, by early afternoon, fed, clean, decently clad in a posy-print house-dress, the cut on my face patched with sticking-plaster, I paced my room, fretting.

Pertelote's voice echoed within my mind: *Flora. You are to kill no one ever again. What 'ave you done with Dr. Watson?*

Dear heavens, I needed to find out.

If I were to help Dr. Watson—if he were yet alive!—I desperately needed to know more about Flora. Her last name. Whether she had ever really killed anyone. Whether she had really been committed, and whether Dr. Watson had signed the order, giving her a motive to take revenge upon him. And I needed to find out the exact procedure for having a person put away; I knew only that it required the signatures of a family member and a couple of medical doctors on some papers. With my various questions I needed to go to the borough office, the police, the lunatic asylum, Colney Hatch itself, and investigate—

But with a cut, however superficial, on my face, I could not possibly go as the beautiful Miss Everseau. Even the merest pimple would have kept such a lady in seclusion until it healed.

Yet I had no other disguise available to me here, not even a full veil. And even if I had, it would have been of small help, for only the lovely Miss Everseau, in my experience, could wheedle information out of officialdom.

Until the scratch above my mouth healed—no matter how much I moved about my room, I could not run away from this inexorable fact—until my face healed or I found a suitable disguise for it, I could do nothing.

I could not even leave my lodging when anyone might see me.

Intolerable. What might happen to Dr. Watson in the meantime?

What might already have happened to him?

"Confound everything! This will not *do*!"

Leave Watson to Flora's dubious mercies for even a day longer? I would never be able to face myself in the mirror again if I did so. Yet I could see no other option, except . . .

Except to communicate with my brother Sherlock.

And the very thought threw me instantly into a terror. The idea of going to see him was simply out of the question. Even supposing I sent him a message; he was so clever, how easily he might trace it back to me! To judge by the accounts I heard of Sherlock Holmes, anything—my choice of stationery, the colour of my ink, something about my handwriting, a postman's fingerprint—any trifle might betray me to him.

I simply could not risk it.

Yet I had to.

If I did nothing, and Dr. Watson died . . .

"Piper, ma'am," came the timid voice, along with an equally timid knock at my door, of the girl-of-all-work, whom I had sent out for a *Pall Mall Gazette*.

"Thank you. Just leave it on the stand, please."

Once she had departed, I fetched the paper into my room and, still pacing, I scanned it for any further news of Dr. Watson. There was, of course, none. Impatiently tossing the rest of the newspaper away, I turned next to the "agony columns." As I rather expected—for it had appeared every day since the first time I had seen it—there I found once again.

422555 415144423451 33424454235154535 1
3532513451 35325143 23532551
55531534 3132345
5441143543251331533.

Deciphered: *IVY DESIRE MISTLETOE WHERE WHEN LOVE YOUR CHRYSANTHEMUM.*

And still I did not know what to do.

I knew my mother. She was simply not the "love" sort. She would not have sent for me.

Yet how I wished she had. Especially now, when I was

so worried about Dr. Watson. Mother would know what to do. I felt sure she would.

If by the tiniest unlikely possibility this message *had* come from her—could I let the chance go by? If she had extended the hand of familial affection to me now, and if I did not respond, would she extend it ever again?

Perhaps she intuited that I might be a trifle upset with her, and she wished to make amends?

Yet my mother—WHERE WHEN—surely Mother, being the one who had to travel into London, from the Gypsies only knew where, would prefer herself to set the time and meeting place?

Might it be that someone did not wish to make me suspicious by naming the wrong sort of place?

While thoughts such as these ran through my mind—circled, rather, like a dog chasing its tail—my eyes went about their own business, scanning onwards into the "agony columns," where nothing particularly demanded their scrutiny until they happened upon a quite arresting, and mysterious, "personal" all in capital letters:

ALONE PART PART ALONE

Unattributed and unsigned.

ALONE PART PART ALONE

That was all.

I peered at it, bewildered, as I am sure a great many other

readers were, by such an enigmatic, anonymous message in such bold print that one could not help but notice it. No cipher either. Plain English. Someone quite wanted to tell someone else something—but what? Part alone? Part from whom? And how otherwise than alone? No difficulty there for me; I was always alone, my very name spelled *alone* backwards—

Then I saw.

ENOLA TRAP TRAP ENOLA

I burst out laughing, enormously relieved. It was a cipher after all, so childishly simple that only a genius such as Mother could have placed it. Thanks to her, I now knew for sure that the IVY DESIRE MISTLETOE message was a canard, undoubtedly originating from my dear brother Sherlock. And I now knew something far more important: My mother might not be motherly in any usual sense of the word, but she did care for me. In her way.

Quite a difficult task, that of assisting my brother to locate Dr. Watson, remained before me, but I felt more able to face it now. Envisioning my mother's face—with warm affection—I calmed enough to sit down. Fortified in my resolve, I took pencil and a sheaf of foolscap paper in hand.

So. What did I need to communicate to my brother, and what could be left out?

First of all, what exactly did I know as fact?

With my paper in my lap I scrawled:

116

I know that Pertelote said "What's 'e done now." Or it could have been "What's she done now," sounding much the same. Meaning the sister.

I know that Pertelote speaks of her husband Mr. Kippersalt as alive, but Flora speaks of him as deceased.

I know that Pertelote told Flora, "Don't plant no more people" ??? What did Flora reply? Something about putting someone in a place that would "do for him." Did she refer to Mr. Kippersalt? Or did she refer to Dr. Watson?

I know that Pertelote asked her, "What have you done with Dr. Watson?"

I know that Flora dressed as a man; almost certainly it was she who sent the bizarre bouquets.

I know that Pertelote told her not to kill anyone "ever again." Did Flora kill Watson?

A most upsetting question.

In between jottings, I doodled, and now I began to draw in earnest. While far from being an artist, I have a knack for drawing people's faces in an exaggerated sort of way, and I have found that doing so helps me think. I sketched Pertelote. (What was her real name? Had she recognised me outside her window? More questions to which I had no way of finding answers.) I drew Flora as a man complete with nose and goatee, considering that she made a much more satisfactory man than a woman, and it was narrow-minded of Pertelote to think otherwise. But how had Flora come to adopt this disguise?

Then I remembered, and wrote:

Flora said, "I 'ad to act the part o yer 'usband, now, didn't I?"
  Pertelote said to let him rest in peace.

Although suffering a certain degree of self-doubt since my theory of Watson and the noseless soldier had proved to be so badly mistaken, still, I began to hypothesise what may have happened between Pertelote, Flora and the missing Mr. Kippersalt. Although attempting to help his wife's sister at first, Mr. Kippersalt had eventually found Flora unbearable and had her committed to Colney Hatch. (While I sat thinking, I drew Flora as a woman, putting features similar to Pertelote's on her.) Pertelote, however, whose life had been devoted to Flora since the unfortunate incident of the hungry rats, could not let her sister be locked up for a lunatic, even though Flora arguably was one. Forced to choose between her husband and her sister, she championed the latter, defied her husband and had Flora released from the insane asylum.

Flora then promptly killed Mr. Kippersalt.

This event apparently had not broken Pertelote's heart. Pertelote had helped conceal the crime by pretending her husband was still alive. Meanwhile she had tried to take control of her sister so that no more such unfortunate incidents would occur. Flora, apparently, still intended to make trouble of some sort . . .

Of course.

Remembering another snippet of overheard conversation, I made a note:

"You'll be sorry! You an' any doctor 'oo signs an order for you!"

Flora still held a grudge against Dr. Watson, who had signed the order to have her put away. Surely I had hit upon the truth of the matter.

But—what had she done to him? Killed him?

The thought sent a chill through me, and a pang to my heart. I hesitated to accept it.

Musing, I sketched Flora as I had seen her, nose and face putty torn off. But it was hard—painful, I mean—to depict her that way, poor woman. I imagined two Cockney children, on their own in the most abject poverty while their mother scrubbed some more fortunate woman's floor—or perhaps their mother was dead already. Or perhaps she had beaten and ceased to love the older child when she had come home to find the younger one's face eaten off by rats. Or perhaps she had ceased to love the disfigured one. Mother or no mother, growing up that way, so disfigured, was enough to make anyone insane.

Shuddering, I looked down at my drawing to find that in my sympathy, or perhaps in a sort of understanding beyond logic, I was turning Flora to flowers.

I had given her a convolvulus mouth, an upside-down rosebud for a nose, and now I went on to give her poppies for eyes, and for hair, asparagus fronds, of course, wild and stringy. She made quite a bizarre bouquet.

Ye gods in white nightgowns, I was back where I had started.

All of the flowers except the rose—which, upside down, symbolised the opposite of love—had been in the original bouquet I had seen in Mrs. Watson's parlour.

And I quite understood all of them except the asparagus. What on earth was the meaning of asparagus?

For the matter of that, why did Flora grow so very much asparagus in her hothouse?

For bouquets? She had enough fronds for a thousand. To eat? She could have supplied all of Holywell Street, but I had seen no evidence that any spears had ever been cut—

Spears.

That might be it, I reflected. A spear, a stabbing weapon: hatred or death. Why, the name of the plant itself included the sentiment in a way; a-spear-a-gus—

Spear of Gus.

I sat straight up with a cry, scattering papers left and right, for in that moment of blazing-white electric-search-light illumination I saw it all, I understood everything, seemingly insurmountable difficulties fell away, and I knew exactly what to do.

CHAPTER
THE
SIXTEENTH

THERE WOULD BE NO NEED, AFTER ALL, to risk my freedom by writing a letter to my brother Sherlock.

Instead, nearly giddy with excitement, I seized upon a fresh piece of paper and began to compose a communication of another sort.

Several moments later, I finished, thus:

> *5453411155 43535343 315323435155*
> *3211543132 114455231533 114413 125334 3334*
> *1342141451344112354. E.H.*

I did not allow myself to hesitate over my bravado in signing this with my own initials. I daresay I resembled my brother Sherlock not only nasally but in other ways; it seemed that, like him, I needed to have my little moments of drama.

And surprise. For which reason, I have withheld from you, gentle reader, the sense of the above message at this time, and while I am sure you are capable of deciphering it, I hope you will refrain for the few remaining pages of this narrative.

Once I had inked a final copy of my cipher, blotted it, folded it and sealed it with wax, I considered how best to convey it to the *Pall Mall Gazette*, as soon as possible so that it would appear in tomorrow morning's edition. I could not possibly trust this important errand to some street urchin. But a uniformed messenger boy or a licensed commissionaire could be questioned and traced back to me. Eventually, rolling my eyes, I realised I was on my own, as usual, and rose to see about it. With a combination of pencil and "recondite emollient" I coloured the sticking plaster on my face to be, I hoped, less noticeable, at least after dark—I could not have attempted this undertaking in daylight. But at nightfall, in my rusty-black dress and shawl, wearing my wig and my most wide-brimmed face-shadowing hat with a strip of veil attached for good measure, I ventured forth to Fleet Street.

All went well. An indifferent night-clerk who hardly looked at me took my money and my message, promising to send it straight along to the printing press.

Good. But I knew that, if I returned to my lodging now, ordered supper like a sensible young lady, and prepared for slumber, I would not be able to sleep. I still felt electrified through and through with anticipatory excitement, plus worry—about Dr. Watson. If he was where I deduced he was, he would survive this one additional night, and all would be well. Over and over again I reviewed my reasoning with the same conclusion. Yet I could not seem to find confidence in my own mental ability. What if I were overlooking something? What if I were mistaken? What if I were a stupid, blundering girl who should have run straight to the great Sherlock Holmes, a man of action, and let him handle everything?

I could not bear to go back to my room and wait. Instead, emboldened by the dagger riding in my corset and feeling myself to be a sufficiently inconspicuous figure in the dark, I made my way back into the "abominable little labyrinths of tenements crowded and huddled up together, to the perpetual exclusion of light and air, and the consistent fostering of dirt, disease and vice . . . the stifling courts, lanes, yards and alleys shouldering one another and cabining, cribbing, and confining whole nests of poverty-stricken inhabitants," as the *Penny Illustrated Paper* would have it—in other words, to the neighbourhood behind Holywell Street, where that morning I had seen a girl wearing a pinafore with no dress under it, her bare feet blue with cold.

At this time of night the streets swarmed with half-drunken men and women, street vendors hawking cheap shellfish or ginger beer or sweets, and on every block a painted female selling something else. And beggars—entertainers, some would have preferred to be called. I stopped to watch a grubby man who had trained a rat to stand on its hind legs in his hand whilst he plied a white handkerchief to make it represent in quick succession a Roman senator in toga, an Anglican clergyman in alb, then a white-wigged barrister, and with the addition of a second handkerchief, a lady being presented at court. He attracted a laughing crowd which dispersed like smoke the instant he pulled off his cap; I was the only one to give him a penny. Then I went off to find the children left behind—or left entirely—by their gin-seduced parents.

It had been too long since I had ministered to London's poor. Not just days, but weeks.

Finding ragged boys huddled together under an archway like puppies, lacking food to offer them, I gave each a shilling—and then had to run away because they sprang up to alert every other little vagabond on the street; had I not hidden myself I would have been mobbed, my pockets ripped off.

So it went throughout most of the night. Eventually I was able to locate the girl I most wanted to find, shivering in her pinafore, in the area where I had seen her before. Taking her to a used-clothing shop, where I knocked up the proprietor, I supplied the girl with clothing, shoes and stockings as well as money for food. Dazed and suspicious, she gave no thanks, nor did I expect any. Blessed weariness and a certain inner peace were my reward. A few hours before dawn I returned to my lodging, at last ready to sleep.

Or so I hoped. I suppose I did doze for a while. But daylight found me wide awake, dressing with care so as to be prepared for any contingency—money, dagger, bandaging, biscuits, sewing-kit, pencil and paper, latch-keys, smelling-salts, headscarf, spare stockings in my bosom enhancer, plus a clean handkerchief, gloves, more money and—I hoped never to forget again—some sweets in my pockets. Despite my best efforts to be calm and efficient, I found myself in such a nervous state that I could barely touch the breakfast the girl brought up for me.

Well before it was time, I hovered, wigged and hatted but unable to sit, at the window from which I could view the Watson residence across the street.

I watched the parlour-maid come out with a bucket of soapy water, get down on her knees and scrub the stone steps white, as she did every weekday morning.

It was going to be a while. Sighing, I forced myself to sit down. With my fingertips I played imaginary melodies upon the windowsill as if it were a piano. Or perhaps I should say imaginary disharmonies, for I have never taken a piano lesson in my life.

The milkmaid passed, as usual, but leading a donkey—not as usual; someone on the street must be so ill as to require fresh, warm donkey milk.

I studied the humble creature as if I had never seen such a long-eared animal before.

After milkmaid and donkey had passed from sight, I drummed with my fingertips on the windowsill some more.

The Watson family's parlour-maid, who had long since finished scrubbing the steps, came out again to give similar attention to the windowpanes.

The ice-man's wagon trundled around the corner, drawn by a wise old nag which stopped at each house on its own whilst its master made deliveries. During the considerable length of time it took them to progress through the street, I watched with fullest attention to every detail, including the colour of the horse; not content today with "grey" or "bay," I decided it was a "roan."

The ice-man and his grizzled nag disappeared from view. My fingers became tired of tapping and lay still. No longer in a state of fevered anticipation, but feeling a leaden ache of longing, I waited.

And waited.

And scarcely noticed at first the barouche that rattled in from the north, for I was expecting a cab. Idly I watched the carriage, which had its top down, as it rolled near, expecting that it might carry some elderly lady, accompanied by nurse, out for a daily airing. Now I could see the passengers—

I shot to my feet and screamed with joy at the same time as I clapped both hands over my mouth as if my brother might hear me.

Not, to my astonishment, my brother Sherlock.

Unmistakable with his top-hat and monocle, his heavy gold watch-chain draped across an ample expanse of silk waistcoat, it was my other brother, Mycroft!

The one who did not trouble himself to look for me, only sat on his throne and gave orders. The one whose customary orbit of home, government office and Diogenes Club never varied. The one who could not be bothered.

Or such had been my previous suppositions.

Quite mistaken. Evidently Mycroft *had* tried to find me; he had come closer than Sherlock to mastering the floral code Mother and I used, and had come perilously close to understanding what would lure me in: for plainly it was he who had placed in the *Pall Mall Gazette* the cipher reading *IVY DESIRE MISTLETOE WHERE WHEN LOVE YOUR CHRYSANTHEMUM.*

As evidenced by the fact that it was he who had responded to my reply:

> 5453411155 43535343
> 315323435155 3211543132
> 114455231533 114413
> 125334 3334 13421414513444112354. *E.H.*

And now, gentle reader, you shall know the meaning of this, if you have not already yourself deciphered it, thus: Arrange the alphabet into five lines of five letters each, excluding Z. In the cipher, the first two numbers refer to the fifth letter of the fourth line, T. Then, fifth letter of the third line, O. Fourth letter of the first line, D. First letter of the first line, A. Fifth letter of the fifth line, Y.

TODAY.

In full: *TODAY NOON COLNEY HATCH ASYLUM ASK FOR MR KIPPERSALT.*

Signed, *E.H.*

This was the summons Mycroft had read in this morning's edition of the *Pall Mall Gazette*—a summons he could hardly refuse, no matter how much it puzzled him.

I could only imagine what had happened when Mycroft

had arrived at Colney Hatch and "Mr. Kippersalt" had been brought forth. But obviously the imperious Mr. Holmes—either of my brothers, quintessentially upper-class and accustomed to being obeyed, could have filled that role—Mycroft had prevailed in liberating "Mr. Kippersalt," for there in the other side of the barouche, as it pulled up to his home, sat—yes—eureka, I had got it right! The other man was definitely Dr. Watson.

The kindly physician himself, looking a bit less than jaunty, as was understandable considering his recent ordeal, but plainly alive and whole.

And widely smiling.

The scene that followed could not have been more satisfactory to this observer. Alerted by the parlour-maid's scream as she saw who was in the open carriage approaching the house, Mrs. Watson hurtled out of the front door and dashed on flying feet down the steps. As Dr. Watson rather shakily emerged from the barouche, his wife embraced him right there on the pavement.

Even better: Here came a hansom cab with horse most illegally at the gallop, and as the conveyance jolted to a halt, out of it sprang a tall, whip-thin man who shook his old friend's hand again and again. Never have I seen my brother Sherlock happier.

Grinning with delight even as my heart ached—a familiar bittersweet feeling, that of enjoying affection from afar—I watched until they all went inside, the cab and the barouche drove away, and it became apparent that the moment of drama was over.

Then, still smiling but with a sigh, I set about packing my bags. It was time for me to return to my room in the humbler, but more distant and secure, residence of Mrs. Tupper.

CHAPTER
THE
SEVENTEENTH

IN THE NEXT EDITION OF THE *Pall Mall Gazette* I noticed the following in the personal advertisements:

> *To E.H.: Yours are the laurels. We humbly thank you.*
> *S.H. & M.H.*

What? How surprising, and how very gratifying!

Comfortable in my old room at Mrs. Tupper's, in a dressing-gown, with my feet propped on a hassock, I read it again: *To E.H.: Yours are the laurels. We humbly thank you. S.H. & M.H.*

I felt quite a foolish smile take charge of my patched-up face as I enjoyed this most unexpected acknowledgement.

Quite handsome of my brothers, I thought, to take any notice of me in the matter, which had been simple enough once I had understood about the asparagus.

A spear of Gus.

Gus being short for Augustus.

Who could be none other than Augustus Kippersalt. Upon first finding the name of Augustus Kippersalt in the borough record-books I had dismissed him from my mind, as he had recently been sent to a lunatic asylum, and so, I had thought at the time, could not be the Mr. Kippersalt I was seeking.

In a sense I had been correct, as the Mr. Kippersalt I was seeking no longer existed.

But Pertelote's husband *had* been Augustus Kippersalt.

Who, I realised because of my interesting experience lying amidst a great deal of asparagus and my even more interesting asparagus-related insight, did not reside in Colney Hatch at all. In fact, I would wager my nose that he was "planted" in quite an oversized hothouse box. I believed this so strongly that—a trifle regretfully, for I rather liked Pertelote—I had sent to Inspector Lestrade of Scotland Yard an anonymous note detailing my suspicions and suggesting that he might want to check into the matter.

As the murder of Augustus Kippersalt had been concealed, no death certificate had ever been filed.

So, as he was still legally alive, Mr. Kippersalt might be declared mad. How Flora had forged the paperwork I did not know and might never know. Neither did I know how she—probably disguised as a man—had lured Dr. Watson out of his club, or upon what pretext she had arranged for the "body snatchers" to put him away. But in essence, it was obvious to me how she had taken her revenge.

"I put 'im where 'e put me," she had said, or something

of the like, to her sister whilst I listened from outside the window. "The place'll do for 'im."

I imagined that being confined to Colney Hatch for any length of time might indeed have "done for" Dr. Watson, but I hoped that, having spent only a week there, he had come to no great harm.

It was perhaps fortunate that I had cut my face, as this circumstance kept me from acting too soon, and thereby perhaps giving myself away.

Not until nearly a fortnight later—well after Dr. Watson had resumed the routine of his medical practice—did the lovely Miss Everseau once again pay a social call upon the gentle-hearted Mrs. Watson.

With my "recondite emollients" subtly disguising my almost-healed face and with my little birthmark glued to my temple, with my wig in quite a stylish coif secured over my own incorrigible hair and with the very latest in hats pinned to the front of the wig, I daresay I looked fetching, if not positively divine, in lace-trimmed buttercup-and-cream mousseline. For this occasion I carried a bouquet of primrose, apple blossom and mignonette: primrose for happiness yet to come, apple blossom for good health and mignonette—I hoped Mary Morstan Watson would understand the mignonette as expressing my very high estimation of her. The mignonette itself is an unassuming little blossom, but it gives off the sweetest fragrance. It is a gift for a person of remarkable virtue hidden by equally remarkable modesty.

As I stood once more on her well-scrubbed doorstep and

sent in my calling-card, *Miss Viola Everseau*, I did not doubt that she would see me, but I wondered whether she would confide in me as before.

My mission, you see, was to satisfy my curiosity. Nothing more.

Although as it turned out, much, much more was in store for me.

"Miss Everseau!" As artless as a spray of mignonette in her meek taupe at-home dress, she hurried to me with both hands extended in welcome. "How very thoughtful, how very exceptional of you to call again! And what lovely flowers!" She buried her face in their aroma before handing them over to the parlour-maid. "Really, you are too kind."

"I beg to disagree. I believe you to be a woman who deserves every kindness."

"But I want for nothing now. My happiness is complete; I am sure you know, John is back, safe and sound."

"So I heard, with great relief, although not such, I imagine, as to match yours."

"Oh! I quite nearly fainted with joy when I saw him. Please, do sit down! Let me ring for some refreshment." I need not have worried about her reticence; she showed every indication of wishing to tell me the whole story. I needed only to ask her in a general way, as we sipped tea and nibbled lemon-wafers, whether the police deserved any credit for her husband's safe return.

"Not at all. The police confess themselves utterly at a loss in the matter."

"Mr. Sherlock Holmes, then?"

"Even he remains confounded. We have no idea who the villain was . . . what happened, you see, is that a man John did not recognise at all came into his club asking for him, and told him that Mr. Sherlock Holmes most urgently requested his assistance in a matter of some delicacy. John says he became a bit suspicious when the messenger told him to leave his cards, his black bag and so forth behind the davenport so as not to appear to be a medical man—it was an odd-looking fellow, you see, something wrong with his face—but still, he seemed plausible, and of course Mr. Holmes has often summoned John on queer adventures. So off he went like a lamb to the slaughter, and no sooner had he followed his betrayer around the first corner than a constable and some other gentleman leapt out of a black carriage and seized him. Naturally he struggled against them and protested, 'What are you doing? I cannot be delayed; I am on my way to meet Mr. Sherlock Holmes!' Then the one with the odd face said, 'You see how it is?' and the constable said, 'Yes, indeed. Classic monomania. Come along, Mr. Kippersalt.'"

"Kippersalt?" I exclaimed, playing the part of one who knew nothing of the matter. "Have I not recently seen that name mentioned in the news?"

"Yes, it was the name of that man who seems to have been murdered and buried in a hothouse."

"Might there be a connection, I wonder?"

"Mr. Holmes thinks so. He is looking into it. At any rate these people in the black carriage thought John's name was Kippersalt. He told them, 'You're terribly mistaken; my name is Watson! Dr. John Watson!' but they continued to lay hands upon him, saying, 'Now, now, Mr. Kippersalt, come along quietly,' and when John insisted, a nurse appeared out of the carriage, saying, 'Do please calm yourself, Mr. Kippersalt,' and he felt the jab of a syringe. The next thing he knew he was in the lunatic asylum, and no one would listen to him. The misunderstanding was quite enough to drive one mad, he says, if one were not deranged already."

"How very clever," I murmured, now seeing how Flora had combined Kippersalt's name and Watson's fame to the downfall of the latter. "How very *diabolical*," I amended.

"Diabolical, indeed!"

The maid came in with my offering of flowers attractively presented in a green glass vase, placing it on top of the spinnet. The fragrance of mignonette filled the pleasant little parlour—much more pleasant without any bizarre bouquets in it.

After the maid had departed, I asked, "Is it known who arranged this fiendishly legal abduction?"

"We cannot yet say, but John thinks it was tit-for-tat by some insane person whom he may have committed in his career. When he can spare time from his practice, he is studying his medical records for clues."

"Who found him, then? Mr. Sherlock Holmes?"

"Not at all!"

I quite expected her then to credit Mr. Mycroft Holmes.

But instead she said, "The identity of John's rescuer is perhaps the most remarkable aspect of the entire affair. It seems . . ." For the first time Mrs. Watson hesitated, and I did not press her, for I felt myself to be on questionable ground, ethically. But with a little frown and a lift of her chin, Mrs. Watson leaned towards me. "I cannot think what possibly can be the harm of telling you, Miss Everseau: Miss *Enola* Holmes was instrumental in returning my husband to me."

"Miss Enola Holmes?"

"Mr. Sherlock Holmes's younger sister."

"Sister? I did not know he had a sister." The keen interest in my voice was not feigned, for in that moment I realised how very useful Mrs. Watson's disclosures could be to me.

"It is not generally known," she explained, "for the girl is a worry to her family, very wilful and boyish, indeed to the extent that . . . well, her brothers do not exactly know where she is."

"I beg your *pardon*?"

Mrs. Watson then spoke at considerable length; I will spare the gentle reader her narration of how I had come to be on my own, hiding in London. What mattered to me was that her account tallied exactly with my own estimation of my brothers' knowledge of me: with one enormously important exception, which I uncovered somewhat as follows.

"You have never met this extraordinary girl?" I inquired.

"No! We have no idea how or why she involved herself in the matter."

"You have only just learned of her existence?"

"Well, no, I did hear—you see, my husband confided in me—he had become so concerned about his friend's emotional state that he took it upon himself to contact Dr. Ragostin."

"Dr. Ragostin?" I echoed with appropriate incomprehension.

"The so-called Scientific Perditorian." Her tone carried as much scorn as her sweet voice was capable of conveying. "A charlatan, John now thinks."

"Your husband learned nothing from this Dr. Ragostin?"

"He never even *saw* the man. He dealt only with a young woman who served as his secretary."

"I wonder whether it could be my friend Marjory Peabody," I murmured in absent-minded tones. "Terrible what the decline in agriculture has done to the old landed families, you know. Marjory has been forced to take a position with some sort of doctor. Do you know Dr. Ragostin's secretary's name?"

"I'm sorry to say I do not. I know nothing of her."

"Not even her appearance? Is she fair-haired, and plump?"

"I really cannot say. My husband barely spoke of her; he took no notice of her."

My demeanour as Mrs. Watson told me these words of salvation remained, I think and hope, quite civilised, as did my manner as she continued to detail the mystery surrounding Enola Holmes and her role in the rescue of Dr. Watson. But all the while, as eventually the tale was told and I arose, congratulated Mrs. Watson, embraced her, with fervid good wishes, and departed—a perfect lady—during all of this my mind, like a dirty-faced child, leapt and shrieked, turned cartwheels and displayed the most immodest hand-stands whilst joyously yelling: Hooray for the simple, good-hearted Dr. Watson!

A few weeks ago I had written on a list:

He (my brother Sherlock) knows I use the first name Ivy.

One must assume that he now knows from Dr. Watson that a young woman named Ivy Meshle worked for the world's first and only Scientific Perditorian.

But from what Mrs. Watson had just said, one must assume nothing of the sort!

Unless—could she have been coached to say this to entrap me?

No, I felt sure not. It was simply not logically possible, for no one could have known or expected I would be visiting, in whatever guise. Moreover, Mrs. Watson's observations had the ring of truth about them, the tender forbearance of a wife towards a somewhat obtuse and absent-minded husband. As I walked away from Dr. Watson's residence, mentally I invoked blessings upon his kindly and rather dense head forever. Heaven love the man, he attached no importance to Miss Meshle; he failed to remember her last name, let alone her first.

And such being the case, even if he had confessed to Sherlock Holmes concerning his visit to that charlatan, Dr. Ragostin, he had not told my brother anything of Ivy Meshle.

Hence, great happiness to me:

I could be Ivy Meshle again.

I could continue to pursue my life's calling. (Necessarily I restrained myself from skipping, rather than walking at a well-bred pace, as I trod the very respectable pavements of Oxford Street.)

And someday, after I had come of age and could no longer legally be sent hither and yon against my will, someday, nearly seven long years away but nevertheless worth dreaming upon, someday I would pursue that calling under my own name.

Enola Holmes, the world's first and only *real* private consulting Scientific Perditorian.

APRIL,
1889

"FLORA HARRIS," SAYS THE great detective, Mr. Sherlock Holmes, to his friend and colleague Dr. Watson as they relax after an excellent dinner at Simpson's-in-the-Strand. "Or 'Arris, I suppose I ought to say, as she is eminently qualified to a place in the ranks of those born within the sound of the bells of St. Mary-le-Bow."

Only a little slow to follow, Watson nods. "Cockney, you mean."

"Precisely. Flora Harris and her sister, Frances, five years older. Flora did not marry. Frances, however, married above her station. She and her husband started a shop in Holywell Street, Chaunticleer's; Frances took it into her head to start calling herself Pertelote."

"Clever," Watson remarks, admiring a handsome Havana cigar he intends to enjoy in a few minutes, "but a bit irregular."

"The entire family seems to have been more than a bit irregular, as you've discovered to your discomfiture."

"Have I? I can't say I recognise anything you've told me so far."

"The older sister's husband's name was Augustus Kippersalt."

"Ah!" Watson drops his cigar upon the tablecloth and does not bother to retrieve it.

"His wife's younger sister resided with them. A bit of an odd arrangement, I should say. Augustus Kippersalt eventually had her put away on the basis of George Sandism."

Watson sits up straight for a moment of mental illumination and excitement. "I remember now! It was not just that the woman dressed like a man; there were a variety of unsettling indications that she ought to be separated from the body public so as not to infect it. An unhealthy relationship between the sisters, an accidental facial disfigurement concerning which the younger was bitter to the point of monomania—"

"Oh, Flora Harris is a madwoman, right enough. No one is challenging your diagnosis, Doctor."

"So you are saying it was she who—was *she* the man who came and fetched me from my club?" Dr. Watson's incredulity has grown by the moment.

"Yes, indeed. And she who gave you that nasty week in Colney Hatch." Holmes goes on to explain how Mrs. Pertelote Kippersalt, herself also perhaps a bit mad, had chosen her sister over the husband, releasing the former from the asylum at the expense of the latter's life. The murder had apparently upset the older sister, who had kept a tight

141

rein on the younger one for a long time after. But eventually Pertelote Kippersalt's vigilance had lessened, and Flora Harris had managed to orchestrate her revenge upon the doctor who had signed her commitment papers.

"But it's all so absurdly simple," says Watson placidly, once more at ease in his chair, when everything has been explained to him.

"Now, in retrospect, yes. But at the time . . ." A very strange expression ghosts across the great detective's face. As if for comfort, Sherlock Holmes produces pipe and tobacco pouch from an inner pocket of his cutaway jacket. "At the time," he admits in a low, strained voice, "it simply never occurred to me."

"All's well that ends well."

"In your goodness of heart you do not reproach me, my dear Watson, but I reproach myself for neglecting an obvious avenue of inquiry. You would be in Colney Hatch still if it were not for my sister."

Although fully aware that Watson knows of his sister's existence—they had, after all, both been present the night Enola, in a nun's black garb, had burst into Watson's house with a half-killed lady who required the doctor's care—although there has been more than sufficient opportunity, this is the first time the great detective has willingly mentioned her to his close friend Watson. As the touchy topic is introduced, the good doctor is careful not to react, not even to blink.

"Ah. Your sister," he says as if he and Holmes converse about Enola as routinely as they mention Holmes's monograph on the identification of different types of cigar ashes. "What do you make of your sister, Holmes?"

There is a silence which extends for several moments as the great detective stares, focused on nothing within the gentlemen's saloon at Simpson's, his expression most difficult to read.

"I think," he says at last, "that it is a great pity she will not trust in me."

Take a sneek peek at the next
Enola Holmes mystery:
*The Case of the Peculiar Pink
Fan*

MAY,
1889

"IT HAS NOW BEEN MORE THAN eight months since the girl went missing—"

"The girl has a name, my dear Mycroft," interrupts Sherlock with only a slight edge in his voice, mindful that he is his brother's dinner-guest. Mycroft, an excellent host despite his reclusive ways, has waited until the wood-pigeon pie with currant sauce has been despatched before addressing the unpleasant problem of their youthful sister, Enola Holmes.

"Enola. Nor, alas, did she go missing in any usual sense of the term," adds Sherlock in quieter, almost whimsical tones. "She rebelled, she bolted, and she has actively eluded us."

"But that is not all she has actively done." Grunting as his frontal amplitude gets in his way, Mycroft leans forward and reaches for the cut-glass decanter.

Aware that Mycroft has something of essence to say, Sherlock waits silently while his older brother refills their glasses with the excellent beverage that is making this conversation palatable. Both men have loosened their high starched collars and black ties.

Mycroft sips his drink before he continues speaking in his usual ponderous and irritating way. "During that eight-month period of time she has been instrumental in rescuing three missing persons, and in bringing three dangerous criminals to justice."

"I had noticed," Sherlock acknowledges. "What of it?"

"Do you not detect a most alarming pattern in her activities?"

"Not at all. Sheerest happenstance. The case of the Marquess of Basilwether she stumbled across. Lady Cecily Alistair she found while administering charity upon the streets in her guise as a nun. And—"

"And she just *happened* to be able to identify the kidnapper?"

Sherlock stares down Mycroft's acid comment. "And, as I was going to say, concerning Watson's disappearance, if he were not so publicly linked with me, would she have become involved?"

"You do not know how or why she became involved. You still do not know how she found him."

"No," admits Sherlock Holmes, "I do not." Partially due to the mellowing influence of his brother's well-aged port wine, and partially due to the passing of time and certain events that have occurred, thoughts of his runaway sister no longer cause him sharp chagrin and even more keen anxiety. "And it is not the first time she has outwitted me," he says, almost with pride.

"Bah. What good will such tricks and temerity do her when she becomes a woman?"

"Little enough, I suppose. She is a true daughter of our Suffragist mother. But at least for the moment, I no longer fear for her safety. Evidently she is quite able to take care of herself."

Mycroft gestures as if brushing away an irritating insect. "That is not the point. It is the girl's future that is at stake, not her immediate survival. What is to become of her in a few years? No gentleman of any means will wed such an independent young woman who interests herself in criminal activities!"

"She is only fourteen, Mycroft," Sherlock points out patiently. "When she reaches courting age, I doubt she will any longer carry a dagger in her bosom."

Mycroft arches his thorny eyebrows. "You think she will eventually conform to society's expectations? You, who refused to take a degree in any recognised field, instead inventing your own calling and livelihood?"

The world's first and only private consulting detective gestures dismissively. "She is *female,* my dear Mycroft. The biological imperatives of her sex urge her to nest and procreate. The first stirrings of womanly maturity will impel her—"

"Bah! Balderdash!" Mycroft can no longer restrain his asperity. "You really think our renegade sister will settle down to find herself a husband—"

"Why, what do you think she will do?" retorts Sherlock, a bit stung; the great detective is unaccustomed to the word *balderdash* as applied to his pronouncements. "Perhaps she intends to make a life-long career of finding missing persons and apprehending evildoers?"

"It is possible."

"What, you believe she might set herself up in business? As my competition?" Sherlock's annoyance gives way to amusement; he begins to chuckle. Mycroft says quietly, "I would not put it beyond her."

"You'll have her smoking cigars next!" Sherlock Holmes laughs heartily now. "Have you forgotten our sister is just a wayward child? She cannot possibly possess such fixity of purpose. Preposterous, my dear Mycroft, utterly preposterous!"

Nancy Springer

Nancy Springer has written more than fifty books for adults, young adults, and children, in genres including mythic fantasy, contemporary fiction, magic realism, horror, and mystery. She has sold over 2 million copies worldwide and has won many awards. Nancy's books have been sold in the UK, Sweden, Denmark, Holland, Germany, France, Italy, the Czech Republic, Japan, Israel, Spain, Turkey and Brazil. Nancy lives in Florida with her husband.

HOT
KEY
BOOKS

Thank you for choosing a Hot Key book.

If you want to know more about our authors
and what we publish, you can find us online.

You can start at our website

www.hotkeybooks.com

And you can also find us on:

We hope to see you soon!